Murder at the Writers Conference

A Write Club Mystery

Michelle Corbier

Michelle Corbier

701 Green Valley Road, Suite 100, 325

Greensboro, NC 27408

For more information:

www.MichelleCorbier.com

This is a work of fiction. Names, characters, places, brands, media, and incidents are either the product of the author's imagination or are used fictitiously.

Book cover design by Angela Stevens from Cutting Edge Studio.

Murder at the Writers Conference

979-8-9870408-9-8   Murder at the Writers Conference ebook

979-8-9903308-3-2   Murder at the Writers Conference paperback

Books by Michelle Corbier

For Jean-Michel, all my love.

The Brassy Book Blogger

Hello, lovelies. This morning, I knocked out two chapters of my next novel while watching waves lap against the Charleston dock. It's heaven living by the ocean.

Can't wait to finish. The plot explores three sisters coping with the loss of their matriarch. It's set in the low country with plenty of Southern culture.

Back to business. Time to address Fiction Writers of America—FWA.

What is going on with their Platinum Pen Award contest? Since its inception, I've attended every FWA conference. And this year, it will be held in Rock Hill, South Carolina. Great location for a short hop into Charlotte for shopping.

Through persistence, I secured a meeting with their president, Lydia Keller. I suspect shenanigans with their selection process. It's uncanny how often a certain author wins this allegedly open and fair national contest. Who are the judges?

Don't worry. In classic Paige fashion, I will demand answers. The discussion between me and the president will be posted here, on my personal blog. I anticipate multiple sessions, but the first will be next Thursday. If you're attending the conference, reach out. A combined front of concerned authors will let FWA know we mean business.

These transgressions will not be tolerated. They need to make the process transparent and fair. As a longstanding dues-paying member, I will not stop.

On behalf of authors, I will insist on the truth. And if I don't get it, the nefarious activities of the organization will be exposed, here on my blog.

So, touch up your lipstick and join me in Rock Hill. For those who can't attend, I'll post daily from the writers' conference. The situation has become treacherous. Send best wishes to your Brassy Book Blogger.

Paige

Chapter 1

Coral honeysuckle climbed along a trellis anchoring the porch deck. Greensboro's summer fog cleared to a cloudless blue sky. Last night, storms drenched the Triad with torrential rain. Insects buzzed around, thickening the humidity.

Over the years, Myaisha adapted to North Carolina's weather. A significant departure from the temperate climate of San Diego, where she grew up. It took more than a summer downpour to faze her these days.

Hummingbirds fluttered nearby. Fruity gardenias lightened the humid air. Myaisha flung back the living room curtains, opening glass doors onto the fenced backyard.

Boomer, her black Labrador, clambered outside.

Leaving the doors ajar, Myaisha raced back into the bedroom.

Why did I leave everything to the last minute?

Last night, she'd started packing, but AJ came over. The evening drifted into early morning. She had barely slept. But now, she needed to hurry. Deniece would arrive soon.

Ding dong.

Myaisha dashed into the living room, but not before the front door opened.

Deniece entered. "Ready?"

"Not yet." Myaisha whizzed around the house, gathering items. "Where's my—"

"What's wrong? You're usually organized."

"AJ came over last night, and we lost track of time."

"Oh." With a mischievous grin, Deniece rested on the couch.

"Nothing like that." Myaisha scrambled into the kitchen, filling Boomer's food and water bowl. "We were discussing our relationship."

"Trouble in happy land."

She grimaced. "We hardly see each other. He's busy with work and his new business."

"Rehabbing old homes on the side, right?"

"The housing crash left so many people homeless. AJ's making a difference." Myaisha locked the patio glass doors. "I miss him—us."

Deniece crossed her legs. "Tell him."

"I have. But it's selfish to take him away from building homes for people with housing insecurity."

"You have needs."

"Mine can wait."

"Instead of *telling* him how you miss him, show him." Deniece joined her at the kitchen island and lightly bumped Myaisha with her hip. "I could give you some advice."

Myaisha shook her head. "Thanks, but I can get my point across without lace panties and leather boots."

Deniece shrugged. "Puritan."

"Can we not do this now? I need to finish packing."

"Uncomfortable discussing sex with your best friend?" Deniece's brow arched.

"I'm not uncomfortable." Myaisha cleaned Boomer's food and water dishes.

"All I'm suggesting is to communicate better with AJ about your wants and desires. Relationships are work. Don't take each other for granted."

Myaisha dashed into the laundry room. She returned a minute later, searching around the kitchen. "Where's Boomer's leash?"

Deniece located it on a nearby stool. "Tell AJ you need intimacy."

A loud braking noise from outside brought their attention to the foyer.

"AJ's here," Myaisha said before sprinting into the bedroom.

Knock, knock.

"What happened to my adorable, organized physician? Today, you're a wreck."

Myaisha returned, dragging two suitcases. "I had to find someone to cover my practice, and this is the first time I'm leaving Boomer with a stranger."

On the wooden floors beside the sliding glass doors, the black Labrador lazily regarded each woman.

"AJ isn't a stranger." Deniece headed toward the front door.

"Boomer doesn't like him."

"He doesn't like any man near his mommy." Deniece chuckled and opened the front door.

Zoey, a brown Labrador, rocketed across the threshold.

"Whoa." Deniece scrambled aside. "Someone's happy to be here."

"Good morning." AJ entered and kissed Deniece's cheek.

Next to the sliding glass doors, the Labs circled and sniffed each other.

Myaisha leashed Boomer. "Morning," she said, addressing AJ. He kissed her lightly on the lips.

Boomer growled.

AJ regarded the Lab. "Still not happy to see me?"

Fur raised along Boomer's back as his growl deepened.

"Stop." Myaisha stomped her foot. "Sit."

After a brief hesitation and a glare from Myaisha, Boomer obeyed.

"Listen." She kneeled beside the Lab, ruffling his fur. "Mommy's going to be away for a conference. I expect you to behave."

Boomer pulled away.

Myaisha held his face between her hands. "Understand?"

The Lab snorted and lowered its head.

AJ reached for the leash. "We're gonna have a great time. Right, big guy?"

Baring his teeth, Boomer snapped at the fireman.

"No." Myaisha shook her finger at the dog.

A chastised Boomer allowed AJ to lead him toward the front door. Zoey trotted alongside them. Myaisha and Deniece exited the house behind him.

"You two ready to go?" AJ asked.

"Almost." Deniece rolled her eyes.

Myaisha returned a tense glare.

AJ unleashed Boomer. Both Labs leaped into the back seat of a double-wide truck parked beside the mailbox. Wrapping his muscular arms around Myaisha's waist, AJ pulled her close.

"I'm going to miss you." He nuzzled her neck.

"Will you?"

"Five long days."

Myaisha hugged him, inhaling wood and sealant, which seemed to have seeped into his skin. Rehabilitating homes had physically become part of him. AJ released her after another peck on the lips.

How can I selfishly demand more time from him?

"Call me if there's a problem with Boomer."

"He only acts aggressive around you. At my place, he's fine."

Myaisha searched his face as if measuring his veracity. His gentle brown eyes and warm smile provided the assurance she needed.

"Don't worry." AJ saluted Deniece. "Y'all drive safely."

"We will." Deniece lugged a medium-sized suitcase to the back of her SUV.

Less than a minute later, AJ drove off.

Deniece loaded the last suitcase. "Can we go?"

"One second." Myaisha bolted inside the ranch house. "I forgot my hat."

Once Myaisha secured the front door, Deniece asked, "Now?"

"Tina and Mary haven't arrived yet."

"They better hurry up." Deniece climbed into the SUV. "I don't want to hit Charlotte's afternoon traffic."

Down the street, Myaisha noticed Mrs. Lula comfortably seated on the front porch. The octogenarian's house was the first one on the left when entering the cul-de-sac.

What's she looking at?

From a rocking chair, Mrs. Lula stared up the side street, preoccupied with something or someone.

Myaisha followed the older woman's gaze but noticed nothing unusual. However, from her position at the apex of the cul-de-sac, she was too far away from the side street to be sure.

Inquisitively, she proceeded towards Mrs. Lula's house when a tan sedan zipped onto the street. The driver beeped their horn twice and made a beeline for Myaisha's house.

A grinning dark-skinned woman motioned from the passenger's seat. At the curb, Myaisha waited as the sedan parked.

Mary slipped out of the car. "Sorry, we're late. Someone couldn't make up her mind what to bring." Mary's head tilted toward the driver.

Tina popped the trunk before exiting the sedan. "My laptop died last week. I couldn't find the cord for the new one."

"Whatever." Deniece helped Mary load items into the SUV. "Can we leave *now*?"

"One moment." Tina removed a dish from the car's rear seat. Beaming, she said, "Snacks."

Myaisha ribbed Deniece's side. "See. It was worth the wait."

Deniece hopped in the driver's seat. Myaisha rode shotgun.

As the group departed, Myaisha waved at Mrs. Lula. However, her neighbor appeared preoccupied and ignored the gesture.

A hardness cast over the senior's fierce countenance. The rocking chair froze as Mrs. Lula leaned forward, gawking in the distance. Again, Myaisha tried and failed to identify what had captured her neighbor's attention.

What has upset Mrs. Lula?

Chapter 2

Sunlight streamed through the car windows, warming the side of Myaisha's face. She adjusted her sunglasses and turned up the air conditioning.

"Why are writing conferences held in the dead of summer?" Deniece questioned, observing traffic.

"Should we get gas?" Myaisha checked the speedometer.

"We're good. Rock Hill isn't far from Charlotte."

The SUV glided onto Interstate 85 South, maneuvering around an RV and an 18-wheeler. Once they passed High Point, Deniece set cruise control and relaxed into the seat.

"We should arrive in two hours," Tina chimed in from the rear. She handed up a plastic container. "There's lumpia, pandesal, and empanadas."

Myaisha opened the container. Buttery scents of pastry wafted free. She chose an ube pastry.

Mary gazed out the window. "I can't believe no one else from the group could come."

Tina retrieved the container and secured the lid. "Writing conferences can be expensive for people on a tight budget."

"Is your publisher paying for this trip?" Mary asked.

"I wish." Tina frowned.

"Those golden days when publishers paid to ferry authors around the country are over," Deniece said while changing lanes.

"Not for everyone." Tina flipped through the conference brochure. "High-grossing authors might receive gratuitous trips with substantial marketing budgets." She sighed. "Alas, I am not so blessed."

Mary lightly patted her arm. "Your book did well."

Tina brightened. "Over fifteen thousand sales in the first year is nice but not grand."

Using the visor mirror, Myaisha regarded Tina. She would love to complete one book, let alone publish it.

Maybe this is my year.

"Are you worried?" Myaisha asked Tina.

"My contract is for two books, and I'm behind in submitting the second."

Myaisha's brows raised. "Didn't you submit an outline for the cul-de-sac murders?"

"They rejected it. Not enough drama for the true crime market, I guess."

Covering her mouth because she bit into an empanada, Mary said, "A threesome and a suicide weren't titillating enough? What does your publisher want?"

"Perhaps it was the way I presented it." Tina stared vacantly out the side window.

"Well, this weekend should stimulate your creativity," Deniece said with a side glance at Myaisha.

"Remember, this isn't only about us." Myaisha readjusted her body to face the rear seat. "We're trying to decide whether the Greensboro Women of Color Writing Group should join Fiction Writers of America."

Tina huffed. "What a stupid name."

"What would you have preferred?" she asked.

"Something dynamic. Inspiring. You'd hope a group of authors could come up with something unique." Tina sniffed the pandesal before taking a bite.

"Their talents were wasted writing books," Mary snickered.

"There aren't many writing organizations which include authors from multiple genres," Myaisha said. "Fiction Writers of America does. And Greensboro Women of Color has authors from multiple genres. It would be nice to belong to one national organization which addressed all our members' interests."

"Why do we even need to join a writing group?" Deniece honked at a car weaving into her lane. She glowered at the driver. "Moron."

Mary lightly kicked the back of the driver's seat. "No road rage."

"You want to drive," Deniece offered.

"Pass." Mary slid across the seat and browsed the FWA conference pamphlet with Tina.

Myaisha said, "Writers need resources and community. As this year's president, I promised to expand our access. How many opportunities do we miss simply because we don't hear about them? Conferences, grants, contests."

With over a dozen completed short stories, I haven't applied to the contests I do know about. I should take my own advice.

"I signed up for an agent round table," Mary said. "Hopefully, I can find an agent who represents poets."

"Hard sale," Tina said.

Mary pouted. "Why?"

"No money in it," Deniece said, keeping her eyes on the road. "Agents got to get paid."

A cloud fell across Mary's heart-shaped face. Her mouth drooped.

"There will be agents representing poets." Myaisha glared at Deniece.

Mary perked up.

Miles passed. Majestic, verdant trees lined the congested freeway. Myaisha watched the scenery as her thoughts returned to last night's conversation with AJ. She wanted to be fair and patient. But she did desire more time with him. Perhaps it wasn't about business. Had AJ lost interest?

Should I consult D for dating tips?

"Why are you coming, Deniece?" Tina asked. "Looking for a traditional publisher?"

"Self-publishing works for me."

Conversation lapsed as Deniece switched lanes. "I needed to get out of the house. Distance is good for a marriage."

Were Deniece and Barry having problems?

Caught up in her own relationship issues, Myaisha had neglected her dearest friend. Deniece's earlier comments at the house might have reflected her own marital concerns.

Myaisha studied Deniece's relaxed unconcerned countenance. "Liar. You signed up for an agent roundtable."

Straightening her back, Deniece said, "What good is a best friend if she can't keep her mouth shut."

Myaisha made a face, and Deniece reciprocated by sticking out her tongue.

"Well, I'm looking forward to the conference." Tina snacked on lumpia. "Particularly, the workshops on Strengthening Your Protagonist's Voice, Building Suspense in Narratives, and Authors' Answers."

"Does a protagonist's voice matter in true crime?" Deniece asked. "It's essentially an investigative news program in book form."

Tina scowled. "Good writing always matters."

"What's Authors' Answers?" Mary asked, reading the conference pamphlet.

"A panel of authors shares their writing experiences and answers audience questions about writing and publishing," Tina replied.

"Hmm." Mary nodded.

"Tullulah Bishop will be there."

Everyone stared at Tina, who said, "Famous fiction author."

A quarter of a minute elapsed before Deniece asked, "Is she the one whose book titles are alphabetical?"

"Grafton," Myaisha said.

"Tullulah Bishop has won the Platinum Pen Award more than any other author."

"The what?" Deniece snuck a glance at Myaisha.

"Platinum Pen is the Fiction Writers of America annual author award. All fiction authors are eligible, but recipients have traditionally been literary fiction writers."

Simultaneously, Mary and Tina said, "That's not fair."

"Poetry is always underrated," Mary bemoaned.

"People don't appreciate how hard it is to write true crime," Tina complained.

Myaisha studied Tina, recalling their conversation over Christmas. The hospital nurse had desperately needed a book idea and requested Myaisha's assistance. How desperate had her friend become to publish?

"Tina, did your publisher enter your novel?" she asked.

"Yes."

A moment lapsed. Mary squeezed Tina's hand. "You couldn't expect to win on the first attempt."

Tina flushed. "Sure, I could."

"This weekend is a chance to learn more about Fiction Writers of America and gather resources for Greensboro Women of Color." Myaisha gave Tina a weighty look. "No drama."

Deniece's gaze sparkled. "But if something goes down, girl, we've got your back."

Shaking her head, Myaisha said, "From North Carolina's ultimate drama diva."

Tina side-glanced at Mary. "There have been rumors."

The comment dangled in the stillness as Tina looked at each woman in turn.

Deniece glanced through the rearview mirror. "What's up, T?"

"I met a fellow author online, from Charleston. Paige Goodson."

"And?" Myaisha asked.

"Her writing group has attended Fiction Writers of America meetings since the organization formed."

"Go on."

"Paige believes the award selection process is..."

"Tell us," Mary said, agog.

"She believes the process is corrupted."

Myaisha eyed Tina.

Deniece asked, "Based on what? The fact she keeps losing?"

Tina slumped into the seat. "Paige's blog is vague on specifics."

Myaisha twisted toward the rear seat. "Don't get caught up in someone else's disappointments."

"No problem. I have enough of my own," Tina mumbled.

Mary rubbed Tina's shoulder. "You're tough on yourself."

"It's not..." Tina's chin trembled. "Y'all don't understand."

Myaisha's forehead puckered. "What don't we understand?"

Tina averted her gaze. "Forget it."

But Myaisha couldn't. What trouble had her friend gotten into?

Before Christmas, Tina explained the desperate situation regarding her writing contract. Money had been paid on the guarantee of a second book. However, the true crime author had failed to deliver. Myaisha had hoped the story about the Christmas murder in her cul-de-sac would placate Tina's publisher and fulfill her friend's contractual obligation. Apparently, it had not.

How bad were things? And what might a desperate Tina do?

Myaisha's stomach grumbled. Acid burned her throat. While searching for an antacid in her purse, she worried. How would Tina's situation affect the conference?

I don't want to have to bail another friend out of a dire situation.

Myaisha chewed on an antacid while sizing up Tina.

Chapter 3

Sunshine radiated high in the Carolina sky as they entered Rock Hill, South Carolina. Heat made the sizzling roadway shimmer. Myaisha directed Deniece toward the hotel.

Under an awning in front of the hotel's entrance, Deniece's SUV idled. Due to the congestion and occupied valets, they headed for the parking garage. Gas fumes choked the dense air. After removing their suitcases, they slogged from the steamy parking garage into the hotel lobby which teamed with activity.

While her eyes adjusted to the indoor lighting, Myaisha observed the surroundings. A line of at least fifteen people stretched before the hotel registration desk. People in business suits flitted by, conversing while clutching paper cups. Families talked and joked, lugging suitcases as they headed for elevators.

Unsure which way to go, she scanned the area for directions to the conference. Left of the entrance, a multicolored five-foot banner labeled *Fiction Writers of America* hung over a second, smaller registration desk. Its line extended beyond the hotel's main registration.

Myaisha milled around the lobby. Someone bumped into her backside, causing her purse to drop.

"You okay?" Deniece retrieved the purse and hung it on Myaisha's shoulder. "Looking for something?"

"Bathroom." Myaisha checked the contents of her purse. "Did you get a parking stub?"

"Yeah. I'll get it validated at registration."

"Let's check in with the conference first," Tina said, steering the luggage trolley over to the FWA registration desk.

As they waited in line, Myaisha perused the lobby. Unfamiliar, weary faces reflected traveler frustration and fatigue. Travel should be fun and adventurous. She recalled a hotel stay with AJ a year prior in Charlotte. Unconsciously, a smile danced across her lips.

"Here." Deniece handed her a bag of chips.

"I'm not hungry," Myaisha said.

"Tell your stomach." Deniece gave her a doubtful look and pulled out a cellphone.

In a hurry that morning, Myaisha had neglected breakfast. Tina's treats helped, but now, her stomach growled relentlessly. She shifted her weight between her legs to alleviate pressure on her back. Thirsty, Myaisha scanned the lobby for a water fountain. The clean, minimalist décor and dark carpeting gave a somber, cooling effect, but no visible signage for the bathrooms.

Deniece asked, "Now, what are you looking for?"

Myaisha jiggled an aluminum water bottle sporting the Greensboro Women of Color Writing Group's logo in Deniece's face. "Agua."

"There should be a fountain by the bathrooms."

"I don't remember one."

She continued to scan the lobby. "Ah. I see it."

With her gaze set on the water fountain, Myaisha stepped forward as raised voices drew her attention toward the front of the line.

"We made our room reservations on the Fiction Writers of America website portal," a tallish woman with streaked blond hair asserted. "The hotel registration clerk said our room reservations were cancelled. What are we supposed to do? Our members need accommodations."

"I'm sure we can make arrangements," a sweating woman said, flipping through an assortment of papers.

A dark-haired woman with a hawkish nose asked, "Where's Paige? She should have the reservation details."

"Of course. She's wonderful with those things," a platinum blond woman said, rolling her eyes.

"Don't be a shrew, Rhonda," the dark-haired woman said. "Paige's efficiency has benefited each of us at one time or another."

"Oh, shut up, Joyce." Rhonda twisted a gold bracelet around her bony wrist. "No need to simper when her highness isn't around."

Myaisha watched as the two women locked eyes. The woman named Rhonda had an unblemished porcelain complexion, which stood out against her bright orange lipstick. The Joyce woman wore a short-sleeve blouse with a high neckline, contrasting against her shiny magenta lipstick. A silver Birkin bag dangled off the forearm of the tallish woman whose blood-red lips resembled engorged arteries.

When was the last time I wore makeup?

Maybe if she dedicated more effort to her appearance, AJ would be more attentive.

When they started dating, he didn't seem to mind her simplistic appearance. Had she taken his complacency for granted?

Things change. People's needs evolve. Perhaps AJ needed—or wanted—something different from their relationship.

The woman at registration said, "We might have a few doubles available. Several people reserved rooms but haven't registered yet."

"How many?" the tall blond asked shrilly. "And when will they become available?"

Joyce said, "It's fine. I can double up with..."

Right then, a large crowd entered the lobby, drowning out the women's conversation.

The tallish woman said, "Let's go. They'll call when the rooms are ready."

Rhonda and Joyce joined the tallish woman, and they departed.

"Tullulah doesn't look her age today," someone in the line said.

"Book sales buy a lot of Botox."

Background noise prevented Myaisha from identifying the speakers.

"Tullulah Bishop!"

The shriek came from someone in an approaching crowd. In seconds, a small mob encircled the towering woman.

"Humph. So that's Tullulah Bishop," Deniece said.

Curious, Myaisha forgot about the water fountain. She observed the crowd gushing over the author. Tullulah Bishop dazzled the crowd with a magazine cover smile. She signed books and posed for pictures, sharing quaint phrases of appreciation for her admirers.

"Must be nice," Tina huffed, slogging along in the queue.

By the time they reached the FWA registration desk, Tullulah Bishop and her entourage had departed, encircled by a swarm of admirers.

The sweating volunteer addressed Myaisha, "One moment. Someone else will help you." In an aside to a petite stout woman, she said, "I need to check on those rooms or Mrs. Bishop will blow a gasket."

"Go ahead." From behind a cherry wood desk, a woman rose and greeted Myaisha. Across her sizable bosom, her shirt read *FWA Volunteer*. "Hello, I'm Tisha Newson. Welcome to the Fiction Writers of America Conference."

"Thank you."

"Let me get your names."

Once they signed the ledger and retrieved their welcome packages, they drifted away from registration.

"Wait. I almost forgot." Tisha reached inside an enormous square box behind the desk. "This year, we bought tote bags for each participant."

The linen tote bags depicted the FWA name and logo.

"Nice," Mary said, accepting a tote bag and inspecting its contents.

"There's a plastic water bottle, hotel map, conference pamphlet, pen, and I believe a package of gum."

"Candy," Tina said.

"Same thing." Tisha Newson sized up Tina with a long, disagreeable gaze. "Have a nice conference," she said snappishly before greeting another attendee.

Myaisha placed the plastic water bottle on the table and dropped her own aluminum thermos inside the tote.

"Where's the opening ceremony?" Mary asked.

No one answered as they reviewed maps from inside their welcome packages.

"Tina?" A slight woman wearing a floppy hat with an enormous yellow daisy approached. "Tina de Jesus?"

"Yes," Tina said.

"Paige Goodson. So nice to finally meet in person."

They embraced and exchanged greetings.

Myaisha scrutinized Paige, appreciating the diamond studs dotting her earlobes. A milky pearl necklace encircled her neck. Like the other Charleston writing group members, Paige wore vibrant lipstick in sparkling pink.

"How was the drive up from Charleston?" Tina asked, slightly leading Paige toward her group.

"Interstate 26 is a beast, especially in this sweltering heat." Paige removed her hat and shook her frizzled hair. "Can't wait to have a shower."

"These are my friends and members of my writing group. Myaisha, Deniece, and Mary."

"Nice to meet y'all." Paige faced Tina. "Is this *the* Greensboro Women of Color Writing Group?"

"A small delegation."

"We have close to fifty members," Myaisha said, shaking Paige's hand.

"Quite a sizable group. At one time, Palmetto Writers had thirty members, before people departed." Her voice lowered conspiratorially. "Our members are aging out."

Myaisha frowned. "How do you age out of an adult writing group?"

"By dying." Paige tittered.

Tina laughed. Mary giggled. Myaisha and Deniece shared a concerned look.

"Nice pearls," Deniece said, pointing to Paige's pale neckline.

"A family heirloom."

"Pearls are featured in the Palmetto Writers insignia," Myaisha pointed out.

"I wanted members attending the conference to wear pearls as a symbol of solidarity," Paige said, delicately fingering her jewels. "But apparently, not everyone owns pearls."

"Not everyone can afford them," Deniece said.

"Costume jewelry is an acceptable alternative." Paige faced Tina, giving Deniece her shoulder.

"Anyway, my group is gathering. Palmetto Writers always meet before the festivities begin. Once things get started, people go their separate ways."

"You drove up alone?" Tina asked, scanning the area behind Paige.

"Absolutely. I needed time to plan my meeting." Her head tilted an inch toward Tina.

"About…" Tina left the sentence unfinished.

Stepping closer, Paige whispered, "The award selection process."

"Oh." Tina's chest relaxed. "It's not a secret. I told my friends."

Paige's eyes flashed.

"I…I didn't think it was a secret," Tina stuttered. "You posted it on Brassy Book Blogger."

"True." Paige peered around Tina toward the FWA registration desk. "I'm on edge, unsure who to trust."

"Do you have proof of improprieties in the Platinum Pen Award selection process?" Myaisha asked, observing Paige's furtive gaze.

The Charlestonian's eyes jockeyed around the room without landing on a particular person or object. Distracted, Paige didn't reply. She simply nodded her head.

Seconds passed before Tina touched Paige's shoulder. "Everything okay?"

"Of course. Why wouldn't it be?" Paige gave a light chuckle. "Oh, I see my group."

She departed, waving to a half dozen women standing near a conference room door. "Tullulah, darling. Here I am."

Myaisha watched Paige greet the Palmetto Writers. Distance prevented her from hearing their conversation, but the women's placid expressions suggested they weren't delighted with the new arrival.

Paige first addressed Tullulah Bishop. Joyce hugged Paige, but Rhonda accepted air kisses with a dour expression.

Deniece tapped Myaisha's arm. "Let's check in."

Oblivious, she asked, "Excuse me?"

"Our rooms. Let's check into our hotel room."

Tina led the way to hotel registration. "Did we reserve a suite?"

"A suite with two double rooms and a central living area," Myaisha said, reviewing the email confirmation.

"Sweet."

While the group checked in, Myaisha observed Paige and the Palmetto Writers.

Deniece handed Myaisha a key card. "What's with you?"

"Not sure. Something about Paige's demeanor."

"Love her hat." Deniece pulled Myaisha toward a waiting elevator. "And those diamond earrings were genuine."

"Tina, do you know who Paige is meeting with?" Myaisha asked, slipping inside the closing elevator.

"No clue," Tina said. "I'm not sure she mentioned a meeting location on her blog."

"Hmm. I need to read it."

A grin tugged at the corner of Deniece's mouth. She sniffed the air. "I smell a mystery."

"Uh-uh." Mary vigorously shook her head. "No ma'am. I promised Greg we wouldn't get into any trouble."

"We're not in trouble." Deniece rested her arm across Mary's shoulder.

The latter looked up at her dubiously.

Myaisha said, "I'm curious about Paige's allegations. If the Fiction Writers of America award selection process is rigged, this is not an organization we want to join."

The elevator pinged, and they exited the cab.

"Give me a minute," Tina said, "and I'll email you a link to Paige's website."

"Leave me out of it." Mary strode inside the room. "I'm going to unpack."

"I'll figure out where the orientation begins," Tina said.

"And I'm going to prepare for a new mystery." Deniece's shoulders swayed as if dancing.

"It's not a mystery." Myaisha collapsed onto a sofa adjacent to the floor-to-ceiling windows. "I simply want to know what's worrying Paige and if the Fiction Writers of America organization is legitimate."

"If it isn't," Deniece said, "we'll uncover the truth."

Myaisha worried about how comforting that idea felt.

Chapter 4

Boisterous conversations ballooned around the grand Mary McLeod Bethune Ballroom, named after the Sumter County native and founder of the Negro Council for Women. Myaisha liked to think the humanitarian would appreciate her name being associated with a facility where people from varied backgrounds gathered to share ideas and fellowship.

Inside the ballroom, a central pathway divided over twenty rows of chairs into two sections. People congregated around the room in tiny pockets. A few individuals occupied seats, eager for the evening's presentation.

Myaisha surveyed the room. "Where do you want to sit?"

"Near the back," Deniece said. "In case it's boring and we need a quick exit."

"I thought you were excited about the conference?" Myaisha regarded her friend.

"Just saying. It's easier to leave if we sit in the back."

"Come." Tina escorted Deniece by the elbow to the second row from the front on the left side near the exit. "This is Fiction Writers of America's welcoming ceremony. It should be good."

Mary followed, reviewing the FWA conference program. "I hope they explain the hotel's layout. It's hard to understand where the breakout sessions are held."

Tina took a seat in the middle of the row. Deniece disentangled herself from Tina's grasp and allowed Mary to enter next.

"Go ahead," Myaisha said, motioning Deniece to proceed.

"I'd rather sit on the end."

After a slight pause, Myaisha sat, giving Deniece the chair at the end of the row.

Over the next ten minutes, the ballroom filled. A hum of anticipation rose with rumblings from the attendees. Myaisha checked her watch. The seven o'clock program should start on time.

Her stomach growled. "After this, let's grab something to eat."

"Not tonight," Deniece said, reading on her cellphone. "Let's order room service."

She glanced at the cellphone screen, but Deniece turned it over.

Myaisha frowned. "Problem?"

"Nope." Deniece stared straight ahead.

"Barry?"

"Drop it."

"If you weren't texting your husband, who were you..."

Raucous applause drowned out their conversation. A line of people paraded onto a stage situated at the front of the auditorium. A banner with two-foot letters spelling out *Fiction Writers of America* hung above the stage, framed by silver and gold balloons.

Audience members began rising. Tina and Mary rose and clapped along. Myaisha and Deniece remained seated.

Dressed in a dark blue double-breasted suit, the woman on stage encouraged the audience to sit. Dark-haired with a thick gray streak and square shoulders, her upturned nose gave a superciliousness to her expression.

"Good evening," she said, "and welcome to the sixteenth annual Fiction Writers of America Conference."

More applause and a few whoops.

"My name is Betty Rohrshack, vice president of Fiction Writers of America. Unfortunately, our dear president, Lydia Keller, is ill and unable to attend the festivities."

Scattered sighs and disappointments were uttered.

"Have no fear. As always, Fiction Writers of America will deliver a stellar program."

Sparse applause.

"Let me introduce a few members of my team. Tomorrow morning, the entire board will be in attendance."

From the right side of the stage, two people approached.

She beckoned them forward. "First, the person who individually invites each person to the Fiction Writers of America family. Chair of our membership committee, Hunter Vinson."

Loud applause with a few attendees shouting Vinson's name. Mr. Vinson joined Mrs. Rohrshack and reached for the microphone. She conspicuously slid it out of his range.

Did she purposely snub him?

Because it happened swiftly, Myaisha couldn't discern.

"And the most important person this weekend for you all, or y'all, like they say in South Carolina." Mrs. Rohrshack snickered at her cringy joke.

Irritated by the two-syllable pronunciation of the pronoun, Myaisha mumbled, "Why must non-Southerners mock our dialect?"

"Tisha Newson." Mrs. Rohrshack drew the woman forward.

Mr. Vinson stepped aside so Tisha Newson stood between him and Mrs. Rohrshack.

"Tisha is in charge of conference logistics," the vice president said. "Each morning, she will be stationed at the registration desk. Afternoons, she will coordinate events throughout the hotel. Messages can be left for her at registration."

Mrs. Rohrshack pursed her heavily lacquered lips together. "Now, *y'all* remember, Fiction Writers of America is powered by volunteers like yourselves. I expect *y'all* to use Southern charm when communicating with my staff."

Myaisha flinched each time Mrs. Rohrshack said *y'all*. "She needs to stop with the fake accent," she whispered to Deniece.

"And stop using drag queens for makeup advice."

Myaisha laughed.

"Shush," someone said behind them.

Deniece grimaced and began to turn around before Myaisha squeezed her knee.

Over thirty minutes, Mrs. Rohrshack and other FWA members explained how the following four days would proceed. Myaisha periodically shifted positions to quiet her churning gut.

"Let's go," Deniece said. "I'm tired of listening to your stomach."

"Can't help it."

"Doesn't matter. This is dull. We can get this information from the packet in our tote bags."

"And finally," Mrs. Rohrshack said, raising her arms forward in a Y-formation. "We want *y'all* to try different activities, discover upcoming authors, and make new friends. On Saturday evening, we present the Platinum Pen Award. This is a formal gala." Her gaze beamed across the room as if solidifying her point. "Please dress accordingly."

"What does she imagine we'll wear, cotton sacks?" Deniece asked a tinge louder than Myaisha preferred.

In that moment, Mrs. Rohrshack's gaze swept over them. A person in the front row swiveled around and glared at them.

Deniece bolted upright and asked the person, "What?"

The woman immediately faced forward.

Myaisha rested a hand on Deniece's arm. "Are you okay?"

"Yeah." Deniece stood. "I'm ready to go."

A moment later, Mrs. Rohrshack concluded the ceremony, and people stirred.

Outside the conference room, Myaisha pulled Deniece aside. "What's going on? And don't tell me nothing."

"It'll be fine."

"Tell me."

"I can't."

"We're best friends." Myaisha rubbed Deniece's arm. "You can tell me anything."

"Unfortunately, not. You're too judgmental." Deniece strode away followed by Tina and Mary.

Myaisha stood there slack-jawed.

Chapter 5

T he crowd streamed out of the grand ballroom. Noise from chattering attendees clogged the walkways. Swept along in the traffic, Myaisha clambered to keep up with her friends. She caught up with them in the hotel's main lobby. Music from the bar added to the commotion.

Deniece headed for the elevators.

"Where're you going?" Tina asked. "We planned to grab something to eat."

"On the way, I spotted a barbecue restaurant near the interstate," Mary said.

"Not tonight." Deniece yawned. "I'm tired."

Myaisha adjusted the gray bowler over her thick black curls. "We could order room service."

"Tullulah!" A perspiring woman bolted across the crowded lobby. "May I have your autograph?" she asked, pressing forward a book.

The cover featured an eighteenth-century woman strolling on a hillside with an umbrella dangling from her forearm. Myaisha didn't recognize the title, but the cover screamed cozy mystery genre.

With grace, Tullulah accepted the book. "Of course, darling. So sweet of you to ask."

The Charleston author's signature would have made John Hancock proud.

"Now, make sure you attend my talk tomorrow," Tullulah said, returning the book.

"I can't wait," the enraptured fan said, clasping the book to her chest.

"And remember, my books are on sale downstairs," Tullulah added.

In answer to the fanatic's questioning gaze, Rhonda said, "Fiction Writers of America arranged for the local bookstore to set up a mini-outlet downstairs."

After thanking Rhonda, the woman sped away.

"How nice," Tullulah purred.

"Don't get used to it," Rhonda said in an aside before walking away.

With a surly face, Tullulah charged after her.

"What happened?" Myaisha asked, straining to follow the departing women amid the crowd.

"It's called having a fan," Deniece said, grinning mischievously, "which you would have if you ever finished a book."

Myaisha smacked her arm.

"Don't hate me because you're afraid to publish."

"It's not fear," Myaisha muttered, recalling multiple unfinished manuscripts languishing on her laptop.

Why can't I complete anything?

"There are only four days in this conference," Tina said. "We came to Rock Hill to learn more about Fiction Writers of America and improve our craft."

Mary said, "*I* came to find an agent for my poetry."

"Forget agents," Deniece said, heading again for the elevators. "Self-publish. Keep your money. You earned it."

"No chance," Mary said, shaking her head. "I need guidance."

"There are resources available." Deniece joined a queue for the elevators. "Readers are more open to self-published books. And the process can be streamlined for efficiency."

"What about dinner?" Tina interjected.

"It's been a long day," Myaisha said. "I'm joining D and ordering room service."

"Don't bother. Room service will take too long, and I'm tired of hearing your grumbling stomach," Deniece said. "Go. Have fun." She bustled into the elevator before Myaisha could reply.

For a few seconds, Myaisha stood gaping at the closed elevator doors. The drive from Greensboro hadn't been long, around three hours with traffic. Deniece usually enjoyed dining out and socializing.

"Barbecue it is." Mary started toward the hotel exit.

"If the point is to learn about the conference," Myaisha said, "we should eat at the hotel. Interact with the Fiction Writers of America Conference attendees."

Tina smiled. "Sounds good to me."

"Fine." Mary brooded. "But I want to try the barbecue place before we leave."

"Deal," Myaisha said.

Tina consulted the hotel brochure. "There are three restaurants in the hotel. Which one?"

Mary scanned the brochure over Tina's shoulder. "Let's try the one on the second floor. Its prices are decent."

Five minutes later, outside the second-floor restaurant, Myaisha consulted her watch as they waited in a line which extended to the staircase. "The hostess said it would be a thirty-minute wait."

Mary huffed. "With this line?"

"It'll be closer to an hour." Tina checked the brochure again. "We could try the one on the main floor."

"The most expensive one," Mary said, bringing her purse closer to her side.

Myaisha rubbed her grumbling stomach. "We have to eat some-where."

A quarter of an hour later, they were seated inside a brightly lit restaurant with an avant-garde vibe. Gigantic light fixtures hung from the wood-paneled ceiling. Abstract paintings coated paneled walls.

"Those lights look like bent clothes hangers," Myaisha said, inspecting the establishment. She viewed the menu. "The prices are exorbitant."

Mary grunted. "And you're a physician. Imagine how I feel."

Once they placed their orders, Myaisha nibbled on a crostini. She scrutinized the restaurant for interesting characters. Often, story ideas blossomed from ordinary events or conversations. People watching strengthened her dialogue—or would if she ever finished a novel.

"Deniece was right."

"Sorry." Tina gazed at her. "I missed what you said."

Not realizing she had spoken out loud, Myaisha apologized. "Nothing. I was considering what D said about me not publishing anything. Years of writing, but nothing published or submitted."

Mary squeezed her hand. "Wait until you're comfortable."

"A writer is never comfortable. You'll always believe more could be done. Change a few words. Edit another paragraph." Tina chuckled. "But if you don't try, nothing will happen."

"Myaisha needs to believe the time is right," Mary said.

"Wait too long and your passion will disappear."

"I don't believe I could ever lose my passion for writing." Myaisha considered a moment. "But publishing seems like so many theatrics."

"And we know how much you hate drama." Mary's eyes twinkled.

Conversation ceased when the server returned with their dishes.

Between bites, Myaisha said, "I'd like to check out the bookstore. What are their hours?"

Tina slid the brochure across the table.

"After dinner, we should attend the mixer," Tina said.

"I don't want to stay up too late." Mary pointed to a paragraph in the brochure. "There's a poetry workshop tomorrow at eight."

"Why?" Tina frowned.

"Apparently, poets don't sleep in." Myaisha smirked.

A guffaw of merriment rang out in the dining room. They turned to find Tullulah Bishop and other members of the Palmetto Writers two tables away.

"They are a lively group," Mary said, wiping her mouth.

"It would seem so." Myaisha scrutinized the group. Despite the laughter and bonhomie, she detected an awkward undercurrent.

Perhaps noticing Myaisha's scrutiny, Tina asked, "What's wrong?"

"Paige is smiling, but..."

Tina observed the group. "She doesn't seem engaged."

"Exactly." Myaisha sized Paige up.

Though the Charlestonian dined, she wasn't participating in the chatter. Instead, Paige eyeballed the group while touching up her lipstick. From what Myaisha saw, the slender woman had barely eaten.

After dinner, Myaisha, Tina, and Mary ambled around the hotel lobby, discussing plans for tomorrow. Travelers and conference attendees streamed past. The hotel teemed with activity. As Tina and Mary bickered about whether to retire for the evening, Myaisha drifted behind.

Despite the pandemonium, she remained disconnected. Troubled by Deniece's earlier comment, Myaisha wanted time to evaluate her emotions.

"Want to go for a walk?" she asked. "I'm restless."

Mary headed for the elevator. "No chance. I need sleep."

Inside the elevator, Tina chose the rooftop bar button. "One drink."

"Have you noticed anything strange about D?" Myaisha asked.

Mary and Tina regarded each other and simultaneously said, "No."

"Doesn't she seem absentminded. Snappish."

"No more than usual," Mary said.

Myaisha frowned. "Deniece is not usually like this."

"She's mercurial," Tina said. "Watch. Tomorrow, she'll be bouncy and energetic."

With a swish, the elevator doors parted, depositing them on a rectangular rooftop deck. Above, a cloudless sky dazzled with a sprinkling of stars. A refreshing coolness had descended after the searing summer day. People huddled in pockets across the deck, giving a festive intimacy to the celebration.

A trellis of gardenias and carnations framed the walkway, giving off heavenly scents. Myaisha exhaled, appreciating the relaxing evening ambience.

Positioned right of the elevators, an elongated U-shaped bar hugged the edge of the roof deck.

"Let's grab those drinks," Tina said.

Mary sulked. "You know I don't drink alcohol."

"Well, I do." Tina linked arms with her.

Myaisha followed.

They ordered drinks and settled at a table beside the bar.

From a secluded corner, Myaisha spotted Mrs. Rohrshack, Mr. Vinton, and Paige Goodson.

"Look." Myaisha pointed with her head.

"Paige must have left the restaurant right after we did." Tina swallowed her margarita. "You suspect they're talking about the meeting with the president?"

"According to Mrs. Rohrshack, she's ill. They must be canceling," Myaisha said.

Tina shrugged. "I'm ordering another margarita. Mary?"

"Could you get me another soda? This time without ice."

Myaisha rose. "I'll be back."

"Where are you going?" Mary asked.

"We came to learn more about the organization. Who better to ask than their vice president."

Greensboro Women of Color Writing Group members wrote in various genres, from poetry to flash fiction. FWA was one of a few multigenre organizations. But Myaisha would not recommend an organization with dishonest practices. She needed to know if Paige's suspicions were valid.

Myaisha abandoned her Long Island iced tea and ambled over to Mrs. Rohrshack. Animated voices reached her from yards away.

Flushed with a menacing scowl, Mrs. Rohrshack said, "This is *not* a topic to discuss tonight."

A slight breeze tossed around Paige's wispy blond hair. "I arranged to meet with the president this weekend. Her illness will not prevent me from getting answers."

In a lowered voice, Mr. Vinson said, "Betsy, this must be addressed. I've heard rumors—"

"Rumors." Mrs. Rohrshack threw back her boxy shoulders. "From whom?"

"Scattered rumblings." Mr. Vinson angled his head toward her ear. "People are losing trust. Memberships are declining."

Intrigued, Myaisha hung back, sidling up beside a cement pole. Though it failed to conceal her location, it provided some distance.

Through gritted teeth, Mrs. Rohrshack said, "This will be discussed at the fall general meeting."

"Conveniently, *after* the elections," Paige said with a slight incline of her head.

Stamping her heeled shoe, Mrs. Rohrshack said, "I forbid this topic from being discussed during the conference. Thursday's meeting is cancelled."

Sweat beaded along Paige's forehead. "It's your prerogative not to attend, but a meeting *will* take place." With narrowed eyes, she glared at Mrs. Rohrshack. "I'm going to uncover what's going on with the awards committee in spite of your opposition."

Paige bolted across the roof deck and into a waiting elevator.

As Myaisha started toward Tina and Mary, a low harsh voice said, "Over *her* dead body."

By the time Myaisha swung around, Mrs. Rohrshack and Mr. Vinton had departed.

Chapter 6

People rushed out of the Marian Wright Edelman Conference Room as Myaisha bustled to keep pace with Deniece. They struggled to enter against the exiting tide.

"Hurry up!" Deniece pulled her forward.

"What's the rush?" Myaisha asked, trying to avoid colliding with other attendees.

"This is the one event of any interest." Deniece scrambled into a front row seat.

Myaisha collapsed on a chair beside her, taking a moment to readjust her purple beret. "That was like marching to Congress with Edelman to establish the Children's Defense Fund."

"Since when did you march anywhere?" Deniece snickered.

"Don't get snarky." Fanning herself, Myaisha said, "I'm trying to impart a tidbit of history."

Tina slid into the row on the other side of Deniece. "She's excited to hear Tanisha Baldwin speak."

To Myaisha's raised brows, Tina replied, "A romance writer."

Mary pinched her nose. "More erotica than romance."

Deniece gave Mary a side eye. "Afraid of a little sex?"

"A little?" Mary sniffed. "Baldwin's books need a triple X rating.

"She's a best-seller with over twenty published novels," Deniece said.

"One of her books was optioned for a movie deal," Tina shared before dropping the program into her tote.

They chatted about romantic literature as the writers panel assembled on a small platform at the head of the room.

"Tullulah's on the panel too," Tina whispered.

From behind, someone said, "Of course, she is."

Myaisha swiveled around on the chair.

Paige beamed. "Good morning, ladies."

In various degrees, they replied, "Good morning."

"Did you sleep well?" Tina asked.

"I've had better nights. The heat gave me a terrible headache." Paige wore cotton lace gloves with a flowered straw hat that somehow worked with her sparkling pink lipstick. On another woman, the look would have been ludicrous, but Paige had an air of sophistication which made it palatable.

"But she doesn't write romance," Myaisha said.

"Cozy mysteries include a touch of romance." Paige swallowed two pills and chased them with a swig of water. "Bit of an upset stomach."

Myaisha noted the unlabeled bottle.

"Did they work out your room reservation?" Tina asked.

"Yes. I'm rooming with Joyce. Have you met her?"

Tina shook her head.

"She's a librarian. Since we often travel together, sharing a room isn't an inconvenience."

"How are things going with—"

"Welcome," the event moderator said, cutting off Myaisha's question.

She wanted to ask Paige about the scheduled meeting with FWA's president, but it would have to wait.

Once the romance fiction program concluded, Deniece leaped up and scurried over to Tanisha Baldwin. Myaisha remained a second too long in her chair. People swarmed the authors' table like rabid fans of a pop princess. Though she stood in the front row, because of the throng, Myaisha couldn't see the table where the panelists sat.

Crushed by the stampede, she managed to escape to a side wall of the room. People peppered the authors with questions. Some requested pictures or autographs.

Deniece posed for a picture with Tanisha Baldwin while Mary and Tina spoke with another author on the other side of the room. None of the panelists interested Myaisha except for Tullulah Bishop—and not because of her writing.

Behind the authors' table, Myaisha noticed Paige corner Tullulah. During their heated exchange, the women darted varnished fingernails at each other like rapiers. Rhonda stood between them, apparently trying to de-escalate tensions, without success.

Due to the volume of the crowd, Myaisha couldn't discern their words, but clearly Paige and Tullulah had little affection for each other. Finally, Tullulah disentangled herself. Rhonda glowered at Paige before trailing after the award-winning author.

The cozy mystery author took only a few steps before several participants requested autographs. Rhonda stood off to the side. She motioned to Paige, who held up a hand and shook her off. Despite Rhonda's attempts to engage, Paige fastened onto Tullulah.

Myaisha noticed Rhonda's clenched jaw. Undeterred, Paige remained close. After posing for several pictures, Tullulah headed for the exit. When Paige surged after Tullulah, Myaisha trailed them.

At the doors to the conference room, Paige grabbed Tullulah's arm. "This isn't over."

Yanking her arm free, Tullulah sneered. "If you want to keep your pretty face, back off." She surged into the hotel lobby traffic and swiftly disappeared.

Before leaving, Rhonda shot Paige a harsh glance. She mouthed the words, *Watch it.*

Paige flushed. Her hands fisted. "I won't stand for it."

Cautious, Myaisha approached. "Paige, what won't you stand for?"

"Liars."

"Who do you—"

Myaisha stood with her mouth gaping because Paige dashed away. People surged out of the conference room. Myaisha tried to keep track of Paige, but the Charlestonian disappeared into the hotel lobby congestion.

Deniece shook Myaisha's shoulder. "You looked like a gasping fish."

"Did I?"

"Let's go." Deniece hooked her arm with Myaisha's. "I got what I wanted."

"I didn't know you were a fan of Tanisha Baldwin."

Deniece shrugged. "Not sure I would say fan. More like keeping track of the competition."

"You took a picture with her." Myaisha grinned. "Admit it. You're an admirer."

"Of her business sensibility and success, sure." Deniece checked her phone. "Do we have time to grab something to eat before the next event?"

"Are you expecting a call?"

"Checking the time." Deniece walked toward the hotel entrance. *Why is she lying?*

Chapter 7

T hursday afternoon, the expansive Mary McLeod Bethune Ballroom held at least thirty round tables. Each table comfortably seated seven people. The verdant green carpet contained a black geometrical design.

Myaisha gazed around the room, taking in the atmosphere and trying to identify familiar faces. Although she didn't know any of the FWA board members personally, yesterday she had reviewed their online profiles.

Deniece walked next to Myaisha. "I hope things get more entertaining. This conference has been boring."

"Remember, no drama," Mary said, navigating around the room.

"I enjoyed the talk on query letters," Myaisha said while scanning for a table with available seats.

"Why? Are you finally going to submit something?" Deniece said.

Myaisha pinched her arm.

"The author roundtable was fascinating," Tina said. "There's a true crime writers' presentation tonight."

"The conference is only as engaging as you make it," Mary said.

Deniece's head moved from side to side as she mimicked Mary.

Myaisha said, "Tables with four available seats together are in the back."

Once they secured seating, Myaisha set her purse and tote beside her chair legs. Awaiting the beginning of the program, she found herself reflective.

Following Sammy's death, Myaisha often traveled alone. Movie theaters, restaurants, concerts became solo outings after her husband died. Seclusion gave her opportunity to study people. Ideas about story plots arose from daily interactions. A person's hair, outfit, or hat might spark an idea for a storyline.

As the announcer blathered on about upcoming events, Myaisha counted the number of people wearing hats. Over 80 percent of the attendees were female. A couple men wore ball caps, which in her judgement did not qualify as respectable hats.

She repositioned her beret. Perfect for a Thursday. On Saturdays, she faithfully wore Sammy's old fedora.

Myaisha grabbed her tote bag and tapped Deniece's arm. "I'll be back."

"Wait for me."

"Weak bladder. Thanks childbirth." Myaisha regretted those words the moment they left her mouth.

A tiny ripple creased Deniece's forehead. Myaisha's stomach clenched.

Moron.

Deniece had battled infertility and lost. Unable to bear children, her best friend's marriage collapsed. Years of counseling allowed Deniece and Barry to rebuild their relationship. They remarried, but scars remained.

Deniece left neonatal nursing for hospital administration. Child-bearing remained a sensitive topic.

"D, I'm sorry. I—"

"Go. It's fine." The hardening of her friend's jaw made Myaisha's heart sink.

Idiot.

Myaisha rose and exited the room.

Across the lobby, Myaisha entered the women's restroom.

How can I apologize without making things worse?

Inside the bathroom stall, she relieved herself and considered what to say to Deniece.

Maybe it's better to ignore what happened.

"Coward."

"Hello?"

Myaisha froze. She thought she was alone. "Oh, nothing. I was talking to myself." She flushed and exited the stall.

Retching from another stall made her pause. A second later came more retching.

Washing her hands, she asked, "Are you okay?"

In answer to her question was what she could only describe as a torrent of bowel movement. She winced as a malodorous stench filled the air. As a concerned individual—and physician—Myaisha waited. The person might need help.

Pale and sweaty, Paige exited the bathroom stall. "Yeah." She hurried to the sink and washed her hands and face.

"You don't look good." Myaisha studied Paige's blotchy complexion. "Can I help?"

"It's just a virus, and a little chest pain," Paige said, leaning against the sink countertop. "I'll be fine."

Blatant lie.

Myaisha touched Paige's arm. "Let me help you to your room. Sounds like something doesn't agree with your stomach."

She attempted to smile. "It started in Charleston, but I thought it would pass." Paige's eyes fluttered a moment before she collapsed.

Myaisha caught Paige before the ill woman crashed onto the floor. She gently laid her down. Training kicked in, and Myaisha completed the ABCs of CPR.

Faint pulse. Shallow breathing.

She rushed out of the bathroom and yelled, "Help! Call 911! Help!"

Back inside the bathroom, Myaisha tended to Paige. The door slammed open. Deniece and a herd of people rushed in. Things transpired in a whirlwind. In minutes, EMS arrived.

Paramedics placed leads on Paige's chest and pricked her finger for a glucose check. Another paramedic rolled up her shirt sleeve.

Myaisha noticed an arterial-venous shunt in the antecubital area.

Did Paige suffer from kidney disease?

She stored the fact for later.

"Move," a paramedic ordered, shoving aside a tote bag.

Myaisha grabbed it and retreated out of their way.

Paramedics lifted Paige onto a gurney and rolled her out of the restroom. Myaisha followed them outside, watching until the ambulance drove off.

It took a few minutes before heat and humidity forced her inside. Re-entering the hotel, she found the crowd outside the bathroom had dispersed. People strolled past the facilities, some pausing momentarily to gawk.

Myaisha flinched as Deniece came up beside her. They stood together a moment.

Deniece said, "This conference just got exciting."

Chapter 8

Friday morning, Myaisha exited the elevator and headed for the FWA reception desk. Last night, calls to local hospitals went nowhere. Each facility refused to acknowledge whether they had a patient named Paige Goodson. Myaisha hoped to find answers from the conference organizers.

From across the lobby, she noticed a single person manning the FWA reception desk.

"Where are you going?" Deniece asked, trailing slightly behind.

"I want to know how Paige is doing."

Tina folded a paper inside her tote. "You think they'll know?"

Myaisha shrugged. "Maybe not, but it can't hurt to ask."

"Call me if you find out anything," Tina said. "I don't want to miss the agent meet and greet."

"You already have one," Myaisha said.

"It's good to keep your options open." Tina grinned.

"Besides," Mary added, "she's helping me scout for an agent."

"Good luck," Myaisha said as they dashed off.

"What are you up to today?" she asked Deniece.

"Joining you, for now. I might check out a few writing workshops later."

A slight smirk dangled along Myaisha's lips. "Interested in finding an agent?"

"I'm happily self-published." Deniece entwined her arm around Myaisha's. "Let's go find out about Paige."

By the time they arrived at the FWA reception desk, a line of around twenty people had formed. During their wait, Myaisha reviewed Paige's website.

"Anything useful?" Deniece asked, pulling Myaisha forward as the line shortened.

"Tidbits about Fiction Writers of America. Mostly about Palmetto Writers. In the last year, Paige had become increasingly disillusioned with the organization."

Deniece frowned. "Her Charleston writing group or Fiction Writers?"

Myaisha thought for a moment. "According to her blog posts, both."

"Who still blogs?" Deniece chuckled.

Once they arrived at the reception desk, two volunteers were present, and well over a dozen people waited behind them.

A woman with frizzled dirty blond hair asked, "May I help you?"

"Good morning," Myaisha said. "Have you heard anything about Paige Goodson? I was in the bathroom yesterday when she passed out. How's she doing?"

The woman gaped, resembling an owl about to hoot. "Oh. Didn't you hear?"

"I didn't know which hospital—"

"She died early this morning." The frazzled woman glanced at the other volunteer. "Should we make an announcement?"

The second volunteer, an older man, said, "Not unless Betty gives the okay."

Myaisha's brows raised. "Betty?"

"Fiction Writers' vice president," the woman volunteer said.

Activity in the lobby increased. The volume of conversations rose in tandem.

"Have the Palmetto Writers been notified?" Myaisha leaned forward in order to hear better. "Paige came with her Charleston writing group."

"Hmm. I don't know." The woman volunteer froze as if considering the issue.

"If you have a list of group members, I'll contact them."

The volunteer's mouth drooped. "I'm not sure." She consulted her partner for assistance, but he was giving directions to another attendee.

"Why not?" Deniece asked. "Is the list private? We simply want to make your job easier. Volunteer, like they mentioned during the opening ceremony."

Myaisha peeked over at her friend, but Deniece avoided her gaze.

"True." The volunteer tapped on a keyboard and pulled up a list. "I'm not sure how to print this out." She stared as if mesmerized by the screen.

Deniece said, "Turn the computer around. I'll take a picture."

"Smart." The volunteer swiveled the screen around.

As they stepped away from the reception desk, Myaisha said, "Devious."

"You wanted the names, right?"

"Yes, but—"

"I got them."

Myaisha squinted. "Why are you suddenly interested?"

"Nothing else to do. And Paige's friends should be told what happened."

"Did you really not want to come to the writing conference?"

"Does it matter?" Deniece twisted a purse strap around her fingers. "I needed a change. Things were getting stale."

Myaisha laid a hand on Deniece's shoulder. "Everything okay? I mean with you and Barry?"

"Dull, but fine."

"I'm available, if you want to talk."

"To you? Mrs. Boring." Deniece shook her head. "Let's go tell Paige's writing group what happened. We're both familiar with death notifications."

Myaisha hoped Deniece meant their jobs as medical professionals, and not their recent associations with murderers.

Chapter 9

On the second floor outside the Charles Bolden Junior Conference Room, Myaisha waited. Half an hour passed. Staring at the dizzying carpet made her eyes ache. Deniece scanned her phone.

"Who are you expecting?" Myaisha asked.

"What is your problem? I'm checking the time."

In the distance, Tullulah approached. Rhonda and Hunter Vinson hovered close by her side.

In a quick aside, Myaisha said, "That excuse would make sense if you didn't have a watch on your left wrist."

As Tullulah reached the conference room, Myaisha stepped forward. "Excuse me, Mrs. Bishop. May I speak with you?"

Grinning graciously, Tullulah removed a pen from her shoulder bag. "Of course. Would you like me to autograph your program?" The author evaluated Myaisha as if looking for something to sign.

"I'm not here for an autograph. Something tragic occurred." Myaisha came closer. "Paige Goodson died."

"Paige is dead?" Vinson shouted.

Though her gaze fixed on Tullulah, Myaisha appreciated Rhonda's miniscule retreat.

Tullulah paled and stammered. "Well, I...I had no idea."

"Must have been her kidneys," Rhonda said, softly under her breath.

Myaisha scrutinized Tullulah before saying, "I'm sorry to be abrupt, but I figured as members of her writing group—"

"And her dear friends," Deniece interjected.

A quizzical look flashed across Vinson's face.

"You'd want to know."

"Um, yes. Of course." Tullulah fidgeted with a locket around her neck.

For a moment, no one spoke. Vinson swallowed repeatedly, rubbing his thumb against his middle finger.

Rhonda laid a hand on Tullulah's arm. "Your presentation begins in five minutes."

"Right." Tullulah straightened her back. "I appreciate your telling me—"

"Us," Rhonda added.

"About Paige." Tullulah circled around Myaisha and grabbed the door handle. "Thank you..."

"Myaisha and Deniece." She pointed to herself, then Deniece, who stood by her side.

"Both of you have been very kind." Tullulah began to open the door, where the conference room had reached capacity. "Excuse me, but I have an engagement."

"Would you like to inform the other Palmetto Writers?" Myaisha asked.

"We can do it for you," Deniece said, "seeing how busy you are with more important matters."

Tullulah glared at Deniece and flung her head high. "I'm sure Fiction Writers of America will make any necessary announcements." The award-winning author flung the door wide open and strutted inside.

Loud applause greeted her entry.

On her heels, Rhonda followed and shut the door.

Myaisha pivoted around and saw the membership committee chairperson scampering away.

"Mr. Vinson." She chased after him. "I have a few questions."

He shooed her away. "Sorry. I'm swamped. There are several... I'm too busy." Vinson fled down a staircase and onto the hotel lobby floor, blending into the crowded walkway.

Myaisha watched him flee. "Did his response seem peculiar to you?"

"Not really." Deniece side eyed Myaisha. "Unless you mean his running away like a baby seal chased by a pack of orcas."

She smiled. "I like the analogy."

"That's what makes me a great author." Deniece took the lead in descending the staircase. On the first floor, she pulled out her cellphone.

"What's with the phone?"

"Focus. We have a death to investigate."

Myaisha studied her friend a second before deciding Paige's suspicious death took precedence over Deniece's suspicious conduct.

"Who's next?"

Deniece scanned the list of Palmetto Writers on her cellphone. "Joyce."

"The roommate."

"Wouldn't she already know?"

Myaisha's brows creased. "They might be roommates but not friends."

"Call me strange, but if my roommate passed out and was transported to the hospital, I'd be curious."

"Because you're a magnificent amateur detective." Myaisha smirked.

Deniece smacked the beret off Myaisha's head. "Don't be snide. Let's go find Joyce."

Adjusting the beret, Myaisha mumbled, "Then Hunter Vinson. His response seemed more frightened than surprised."

"Fright is a close cousin to guilt."

"Is it?" she asked.

"Phillistine."

"We can fine tune your literary prowess later. First, we have to figure out how Paige died," Myaisha said.

"And why Vinson is terrified."

Chapter 10

Sunlight cascaded through the wall-to-ceiling windows in the hotel's central hallway, creating a rainbow mirage. Myaisha rested on a padded bench across from the Clayton "Peg Leg" Bates Conference Room. Two days ago, she had left Greensboro, hoping to hone her writing skills and join a national organization. In a matter of hours, a woman had died under suspicious circumstances after a public disagreement with the FWA administration.

Todd had once suggested she attracted murderers.

What made me think about Todd?

Myaisha cleared her mind and regarded the dark-haired woman seated next to her. "Sorry to put it bluntly," she said, "but we thought you should be informed right away."

"Paige died." Joyce had repeated those two words for the third time. The librarian's nose twitched as she gazed out the tinted windows.

Is she in shock?

Myaisha patted Joyce's hand. "Are you okay?"

As if entranced, Joyce nodded without speaking.

Deniece sat on the opposite side of Joyce and raised an eyebrow, tilting her head slightly toward Myaisha. She mouthed the words, *What now?*

Unsure how to proceed, Myaisha asked Joyce, "Do you know how to contact Paige's family?"

"Huh?" In an instant, Joyce snapped out of her trance. "Oh. Right. Family."

"We can notify them if you prefer," Deniece offered.

Joyce popped up. "Thank you. No, I got it."

"Should we contact the rest of the Palmetto Writers or—"

"Don't worry," Joyce said while bustling away. "I'll take care of it."

Instead of returning to the conference room where they had located her, Joyce sprinted toward the elevators.

"Where's she going in such a hurry?" Deniece asked, watching Joyce dash away.

"She probably wants to be alone to absorb the information." Myaisha gathered up her purse and tote bag. "Let's go."

"Where?"

"There's a workshop on writing your first novel."

Deniece skipped along beside Myaisha. "I've already written and published my first novel—several in fact."

"Well, some of us haven't, so come on."

The only light in the darkened room came from the slide show projected on the computer screen. In the middle of the presentation, Myaisha noticed a heavy-set man with salt and pepper hair enter the conference room. He held the door open while scanning the room.

"I wish he'd shut the door," she said to no one in particular. "It's difficult to view the slides?"

"Where?" Deniece asked, looking up from her cellphone screen.

"Who are you texting?"

"None of your business."

Myaisha glanced over at the cellphone, but Deniece locked the screen.

"Keeping secrets?"

"Why are you being nosey?"

They glared at each other as the presenter spoke.

"Ladies and gentlemen." The presenter tapped the microphone. "One moment."

Lights flooded the room. The gentleman from the doorway approached the lectern and conversed with the presenter. Myaisha checked her notes, waiting for the workshop to resume.

Again, the presenter tapped the microphone. "Everyone. Please give us your attention for a brief announcement."

Accepting the microphone, the man with the salt and pepper hair addressed the room.

"Morning. I'm Detective Rashan Cambell with the Rock Hill Police Department. We are looking for the person who assisted Paige

Goodson yesterday in the bathroom. If you know this person, contact—"

"I did." Myaisha raised her hand and stood at the same time.

The entire conference room gawked at her, including Deniece. The detective pointed toward the conference room doors, directing her to follow.

"You stepped in it this time," Deniece whispered.

They gathered their items as Myaisha's cellphone chirped. She and Deniece simultaneously read the screen.

Tina texted.

Police looking for you.

Deniece pried the cellphone out of Myaisha's grasp and typed back

We know. They found us.

Close to Deniece's ear, Myaisha said, "I wonder what this is about."

"Who's bringing the drama now?" Deniece nudged her in the side.

The curious reaction of the Palmetto Writers and now the police. A familiar thrill grew in Myaisha's chest. Two days through the conference and already an enticing mystery.

Chapter 11

In the hallway outside the conference room, Myaisha sized up Detective Cambell. The police officer could have been a linebacker for a professional football team. He stood an inch taller than her with shoulders the width of a refrigerator. His stony appearance could face down any tackle. He led them to a cozy nook removed from hotel traffic.

"Thanks for speaking with us," he said. "We won't keep you long. This is my partner."

"Officer Salter, ma'am." This detective had a short, cropped copper afro.

Myaisha and Deniece shook hands with Detective Salter. The former struggled not to stare at his afro. Auburn-haired African Americans were uncommon.

"I'm not sure how I can help," Myaisha said. "We met Paige the day before she went to the hospital."

"We're not interested in her backstory," Detective Salter said.

"Tell us what happened in the bathroom." Detective Cambell folded his arms, took a wide stance, and stared.

Interested but a tad perturbed about missing the writing seminar, Myaisha asked, "May I see your badges again?"

Deniece straightened up and looked at her. Myaisha returned the glance with a miniscule tilt of her head.

"You don't believe we're police officers?" Detective Cambell asked.

When Myaisha didn't respond, he flipped open a wallet displaying his badge. While she read, Deniece copied the details.

"And you?" Myaisha held out a hand for Detective Salter.

With a loud sigh, he presented his badge. "We simply want to know what happened in the bathroom."

Deniece signaled with a lift of her chin.

"I wanted to confirm you were *homicide* detectives." She observed each detective in turn. "Why would homicide want to know what happened to Paige?"

They might have been standing in a vacuum. Time suspended. Nothing existed outside the four of them. Woodenly, the detectives stared her down. With similar conviction, Myaisha returned their gaze.

Deniece broke the tension. "Why do the police suspect Paige Goodson was murdered?"

Myaisha shifted weight to her other hip and waited.

"Ma'am," Detective Cambell said, "you and your friend are interfering with an investigation."

"Rock Hill Homicide has opened an investigation into Paige's death?" Myaisha revived.

A flush spread across Detective Salter's face.

They hadn't intended to share that information.

The corners of Detective Cambell's eyes crinkled. "This isn't an official investigation. We simply need to understand what happened."

"And there's nothing more critical in the entire county for two Rock Hill Homicide detectives to do than to inquire into the natural death of a woman at a writing conference." Deniece smirked. "Please. This isn't our first homicide."

"Excuse me?"

Both detectives lurched forward.

Hurriedly, Myaisha said, "What she meant was we have *investigated* homicides, not committed any."

"But she writes about them."

Myaisha slapped Deniece's arm. "This isn't a time for jokes."

"No, it isn't." Detective Cambell glared.

"Sorry. We..." Myaisha considered how to explain her penchant for murders, then decided against it.

"Mysteries find us," Deniece said.

Detective Salter checked his watch. "We're busy, and you ladies want to get back to your conference. Tell us what happened."

"Sure." Myaisha explained what occurred in the bathroom until EMS arrived.

"Did Mrs. Goodson mention anything about her condition?" Detective Cambell inquired.

Myaisha hesitated for a moment to recall what had transpired. "Paige mentioned having a virus. I suggested it might have been something she ate."

Detective Salter asked, "Why?"

"Because the hotel food sucks," Deniece interjected. "Their continental breakfast lacked flavor, and the eggs smelled funny."

"It wasn't based upon anything concrete," Myaisha said. "Simple conjecture."

A tiny snarl gathered at the corner of Detective Cambell's mouth. "Are you ladies lawyers?"

"Worse. A nurse and a physician," Deniece said, pointing to herself, then Myaisha.

The detectives shared a glance.

Detective Cambell addressed his partner. "Go ahead. Ask."

Myaisha's gaze jockeyed between the detectives. "Yes?"

"Dr. Douglas," Detective Salter said, consulting his notes. "Reflect back on the incident. Do you recall anything suspicious? Out of the ordinary. Something which made you doubt Mrs. Goodson had a minor viral infection."

"If you would tell me why you suspect a homicide, I could be more helpful."

"We don't want to lead you by placing ideas into your head," Detective Cambell said.

Myaisha's lips pursed.

They're stingy with information. Even Todd would have been more forthcoming.

What made her think about Todd again?

Detective Salter asked, "When Paige lost consciousness—in the moment—what did you believe happened?"

Since the police suspected a homicide—or knew a homicide occurred—Myaisha reconsidered the events in the bathroom. As an amateur mystery writer, she designed complex scenarios to kill people. The practical medical part of her brain brought things into a unique perspective. She needed to harness her knowledge and refocus on yesterday's events.

"It happened so fast." Addressing no particular person, she said, "Paige vomited then defecated profusely. The smell was rancid. Food poisoning came to mind because the hotel's food has been horrendous."

Deniece said, "Even a child can make breakfast. It requires effort to mess up scrambled eggs."

"Water." In a self-absorbed flow of consciousness, Myaisha mumbled, "Although Fiction Writers of America provided bottled water in their tote bags, Paige may have drunk hotel tap water, or developed diarrhea from tainted food."

"Giardia, E. coli," Deniece said, in unrequested assistance.

"Respiratory and gastrointestinal infectious outbreaks have been known to occur in hotels," Myaisha continued. "In fact, an infamous listeria outbreak in—"

"Doctor."

"Apologies." Myaisha blinked and snapped to attention. "My mind wanders."

"Did you suspect anything..." Detective Salter appeared to search for the proper words. "Inconsistent with your experience as a medical professional."

"I don't believe so," she said doubtfully.

"But you're not sure." Detective Cambell studied her.

"It surprised me when Paige collapsed. For a person to lose consciousness would mean a significant infection."

"Sepsis," Deniece added.

"Or significant hypotension from volume loss like dehydration."

"She'd been at the hotel for barely twenty-four hours." Deniece frowned. "What virus would act within hours?"

Myaisha's forehead wrinkled in thought. "Certain strains of E. coli."

"Ladies, please." Detective Salter scratched his afro.

"Wait." Myaisha brightened. "Paige stated she'd been ill prior to arriving at the conference."

"For how long?" Detective Salter asked.

"Paige hadn't been specific, but she did mention being ill prior to arriving at the hotel."

"Which means this started in Charleston." Deniece searched the detectives' countenances for encouragement but met two flat facades.

"This has been helpful." Detective Cambell motioned his partner.

"Anything else?" Detective Salter suggested.

"If Paige died from an infectious cause, homicide detectives would not be questioning the circumstances surrounding her death," Myaisha said expectantly.

Deniece tapped a pen against her palm. "It's murder."

"We're simply gathering details surrounding Mrs. Goodson's death. There's no reason to suspect foul play," Detective Cambell said.

Deniece snorted. "Yeah, right. We've heard it before."

Deep wrinkles crept across Detective Cambell's forehead. "Don't go spreading rumors."

Plastering on her most angelic face, Deniece said, "We would never do anything to compromise your investigation, Officer."

Myaisha bit her lip to not laugh.

Detective Cambell leaned into their faces. "I mean it. Your interest in Mrs. Goodson's death ends here. Understand?"

The detectives departed. Myaisha and Deniece waited in the alcove until they were out of earshot.

Together, they said, "Paige was murdered."

Deniece grinned, "Ready, Easy."

Myaisha agreed. "Let's go, Mouse."

Chapter 12

Myaisha grabbed Deniece by the arm. "Come on."

"Where?" Deniece asked.

Pointing with her head, Myaisha rushed toward the hotel reception desk. "We have to get into Paige's hotel room and look for clues, but first, we need her room number."

Deniece planted her feet and abruptly stopped, jerking Myaisha backward.

"What?"

"I thought we came to check out Fiction Writers of America for our writing group."

"Uh." Myaisha stammered and released her friend.

"I'm kidding." Deniece laughed. "But aren't you always lecturing *me* about becoming involved in other people's business? We didn't know this woman. Why this curiosity about her death?"

Like a chastised child, Myaisha's head lowered. "You're right. This isn't our business."

"It's not."

"And getting involved in murder investigations is dangerous."

Deniece nodded. "Correct."

Myaisha studied her friend's demeanor. "We should mind our own business and return to the conference."

"Yes, ma'am."

They faced each other without speaking.

"Fine. I admit it." Myaisha huffed. "I like solving murders."

Deniece's voice rose an octave. "And."

"Danger is exciting."

"Knew it."

"But scary."

They hustled toward the reception desk.

"All your pent-up sanctimonious purity." Deniece snorted. "Solving mysteries is your aphrodisiac."

Myaisha shot her a side glance.

"Don't deny it." Deniece winked. "Give in to temptation."

"It's a homicide, not a romp in the hay."

"Same thing. Simply stimulating a different part of the body."

To avoid further badinage, Myaisha swooped up to the hotel reception desk in front of a family of four, dragging a half dozen suitcases.

"Excuse me," she addressed the hotelier. "We're with the Fiction Writers of America Conference. I'm looking for a friend. Paige Goodson."

With a dour face, the hotelier said, "We cannot give out hotel room numbers. People are entitled to privacy."

"This is different."

"We need to return something to her," Deniece added, buddying up beside Myaisha.

"We can't—"

"Could you call her room?" Deniece pleaded.

"Or I could leave it with you." Myaisha made a gesture as if removing an item from her tote bag. "If you're willing to take responsibility, in case it's lost or stolen."

The hotelier's eyes widened. "Just a moment." She called the room, using a desk phone.

Myaisha nodded to Deniece.

"No answer." The hotelier looked past Deniece, invitingly toward the family of four.

"Once more. Please."

This time, Myaisha leaned against the desk to view the number on the telephone display.

"There's no answer." The hotelier slammed down the phone. "Now, if you don't mind."

"Thank you so much," Deniece gushed. "I'll make sure to mention your assistance on the hotel survey."

The stunned hotelier smiled. "Well, thank you."

Myaisha and Deniece departed. They boarded an elevator, exiting onto the sixth floor.

"Room 653." Myaisha followed the directions posted along the wall.

The instant they rounded the corner, Deniece hauled her back. "Homicide."

"Did they see us?" Myaisha asked.

"Not yet, but they're headed this way."

Scrambling for a place to hide, they dove into a room with ice and vending machines. From a small glass window, they watched the detectives depart. After hearing the elevator ping, they abandoned the refreshment room and headed again for Paige's hotel room.

Orange tape draped across the door in an *X* formation.

"It's not official police tape," Deniece said.

"True." Myaisha tried the door. It didn't open. "Ideas?"

At the end of the hallway, a maid removed towels from a cart.

Deniece's left eyebrow arched. "We could say it's our room."

"What if she tells hotel management or the police?" Myaisha's shoulder slumped. "Let's get something to eat and work it out."

Her cellphone pinged.

"Who is it?" Deniece asked.

"Tina." Myaisha smiled. "They're in the lobby. And you won't believe what she did."

Chapter 13

Once the elevator doors opened on the hotel lobby floor, Myaisha and Deniece scrambled out, zipping around travelers and conference attendees.

Myaisha pointed. "Over there."

Tina and Mary waited beside the hotel's revolving door.

"I thought y'all were getting lunch," Deniece said.

"Here? Ew." Mary's face puckered. "I'm not eating anything in this hotel again."

"Besides." Tina's voice lowered as she leaned forward. "There are too many people around."

"For what?" Myaisha asked.

Tina inclined her head toward the exit. "Outside."

Shaded by a tree, they huddled a few yards beyond the hotel.

"Spill," Deniece said, "before I start sweating." She fanned herself with a conference brochure.

"We got into Paige's hotel room." Tina grinned.

Mary shook her head. "Not we, her."

"Oh, come on." Tina smacked Mary's arm. "It was fun, right?"

"I was terrified of getting caught."

Deniece pushed Mary aside. "Forget her. How did you get in?"

"And when?" Myaisha asked.

Tina said, "When I heard the police were looking for Myaisha, I knew something was up. So I—"

"Dragged me away from an agent round table," Mary interjected.

"Didn't I get you an appointment with a literary agent on your wish list?"

"Yes," Mary said meekly.

"Gratitude."

"You didn't have to push that woman."

Myaisha and Deniece gawked.

"Tina, you hit someone?" Myaisha asked.

"I didn't hit her," Tina said.

"She tripped the woman in front of us," Mary said.

"A minor incident." Tina blushed.

"Tina!" Myaisha exclaimed.

"I bumped into her, and she fell."

Deniece laughed. "I approve."

Tina faced Mary. "You didn't seem to mind while you were talking with the agent."

"I said thank you."

"Then don't throw it in my face."

"Hey!" Myaisha clapped her hands. "Can we get back to how you got into Paige's hotel room?"

"Easy. Since you two were with the detectives, we…" Tina glanced at Mary. "I hurried up to the sixth floor. While the maid was inside cleaning, I entered."

"She didn't question who you were?" Deniece asked.

"Why would she?" Tina shimmied her shoulders. "I walked in like it was my room, gave her a generous tip, and searched the place after she left."

Deniece and Tina exchanged a high five. The former said, "That's how you get things done."

"Find anything?" Myaisha asked.

"Not enough time."

Mary said, "From down the hall, I signaled Tina when Paige's roommate returned."

"Joyce?" Myaisha asked.

"I managed to snap pictures of the room," Tina said. "But I didn't get a chance to check her drawers or luggage."

"You saw potential in this story fast." Deniece patted Tina on the back.

"True crime is competitive. I have a two-book contract with one book published. The deadline for the second book proposal is past due."

Myaisha regarded Tina. Stress wrinkled the nurse's face.

Is this what writing has come to? Assaulting people to cut in line to meet agents and rifling through a dead person's belongings for a story.

"No judgment," Deniece said, regarding Myaisha's face.

She slightly nodded.

Medicine had become rote. Patients insisted on treatments they heard about online or in commercials. Few people wanted to change their lifestyle or improve their health with diet and exercise. She fought with parents about the efficacy of vaccines and lectured them on the dangers of overusing antibiotics, with little appreciation. Insurance companies pushed physicians toward treatment protocols which ignored patients' individuality.

Disheartened with medicine, writing nursed her creativity. Delving into homicides originated with the murder of her college roommate. Myaisha's first investigation involved helping a friend avoid prosecution.

How many times have I been threatened while investigating a murder?

Deniece was right. Sleuthing fed a primal instinct in her psyche.

I wouldn't call it an aphrodisiac, though.

"We need to regroup," Tina said.

Myaisha considered the best way to approach Paige's death. "First, food."

"Agreed." Mary headed toward the parking garage. "I'm starving."

"There's a restaurant on the corner." Deniece led the way.

A sullen look fell across Tina's face. "What if we meet someone from the conference?"

"Worried about competition?" Deniece asked.

"Absolutely."

Myaisha had learned something new about herself and her friends. Tina desperately needed another book to honor her contract. Mary hated risk and sincerely wanted to publish her poetry. Deniece...

Her vivacious friend took a lighthearted approach to most things. But her recent conduct alarmed Myaisha.

Perspiration beaded along her forehead as they crossed the street toward an Asian Caribbean fusion restaurant. Perhaps it was time to reevaluate priorities.

Number one, Paige's death. Two, what troubled Deniece. The second mystery would be more precarious.

Chapter 14

Coolness like an autumn morning eddied inside The Perimeter. Myaisha dabbed sweat from her brow, luxuriating in the air conditioning.

Waitstaff escorted them to a table near the entrance. Spices scented the air with anticipation. Myaisha salivated, glancing at the menu.

"Wait," Tina said. "Can we sit over there?" She pointed to a darkened corner in the rear of the restaurant.

"Those tables aren't being used right now, ma'am," the server explained. "I can seat you in a corner near the bathrooms."

"Absolutely not," Mary chimed in, giving Tina a stern glance.

Myaisha addressed the server. "One check, please."

"I'll get y'all water."

Once the server left, Myaisha said, "Calm down. We understand your position."

"Hardly." Tina's shoulders slouched in resignation.

Deniece scooted her chair closer to the table. "Talk. What's going on, T?"

Tina gazed absently out the side window. "Publishing is my opportunity to leave medicine. I'm tired of nursing."

"I hear you." Deniece squeezed Tina's hand.

"Things are getting worse. People are quitting, retiring early, taking non-clinical positions away from the hospital."

Myaisha nodded. "I've thought about it, too."

Tina regarded her a moment before asking, "Can you afford to retire?"

"My expenses are minimal. Josiah has a college fund. The house is paid off, so is my student debt."

"Well, I can't." Tears welled up in Tina's eyes. "My fault for having five kids and marrying for love."

Myaisha's shoulders tensed. She spied a glance at Deniece, worried her best friend might take offense to Tina's comment about kids. However, Deniece did not appear upset. In fact, she walked around the table and hugged Tina.

"Girl, we can relate."

"Greg and I worry about retiring too," Mary said. "When the housing market collapsed, we were underwater with our mortgage." She patted Myaisha's hand. "With help from friends, I got a side job. Greg had to work extra hours. We won't retire before our sixties, but we won't be on the streets."

"Tina, you're a great nurse," Myaisha said.

"Last week, a patient threw a urinal at me, and an ER doctor got assaulted by a parent because she wouldn't prescribe a narcotic for their child."

"Medicine is bedlam." Deniece accepted a glass from the server. "People act so entitled."

Mary shook her head. "No respect."

"None," Tina said in a soft, faint voice.

Talk ceased while they placed orders and sipped beverages.

Tina wiped her forehead and sat upright. "I want writing to be a full-time job so I can leave nursing."

Deniece raised her glass in a toast. "Heard."

The women clinked their water glasses together.

Myaisha smiled. "We'll help."

"Wonderful. Let's discuss." Tina gulped down the glass of water. "If Paige was murdered, I want to write her story."

Entrees arrived, and conversation drifted away from writing while they ate.

Half an hour later, Myaisha scribbled numbers on a sheet of paper. "Question one: how was Paige murdered?"

Deniece spoke between bites of food. "Because if this isn't a homicide, Tina doesn't have a story."

"Um..." Mary wiped her mouth before sipping tea. "Don't get upset, but are we creating a murder where none exists?"

"Mary's right," Myaisha said. "We have to objectively examine the facts. But if Rock Hill Homicide is investigating Paige's death, the police must at least be suspicious. If the evidence supports no crime, then we accept it and move on."

She glanced at each person in turn, ending with Tina. The latter raised her brow in agreement.

"Second question: if Paige was murdered, why?" Myaisha scribbled notes while the others discussed.

"Motive matters," Deniece said, slurping her soda.

"Are we not going to acknowledge the coincidence of Paige dying before her planned meeting with the Fiction Writers of America president?" Tina asked.

Mary pushed food around her plate. "Would someone kill to win a book award?"

Tina nodded vigorously. "The Fiction Writers of America's annual award comes with a ten-thousand-dollar prize, publication in their national newsletter, and a biographical profile on their website. Announcements in major literary publications and bragging rights alone would boost an author's profile."

Deniece relaxed in her chair. "As a reader, if you go into a bookstore and find two interesting books, one from an award-winning author and the other from an unknown, which would you choose?"

Myaisha looked up from taking notes. "There's no denying a prestigious award advances book sales. But let's start with question number one."

"There isn't a lot of time." Tina's fingernails tapped along the tabletop. "The conference ends on Sunday. If a murder was committed, the suspects will leave in three days."

"Division of labor." Myaisha wrote sub-categories under question one. She pointed at Tina. "You're familiar with Paige's blog, and you know—knew—her better than anyone else here. Talk to her writing group members and her roommate..." Myaisha frowned.

"Joyce," Deniece added.

"Right. Speak with Joyce. Paige might have shared information about her illness."

Traffic in the restaurant increased. The server refilled their drinks and departed.

Tina said, "I'll learn their perspective on Paige's death."

"Too bad Todd or Ian weren't here," Deniece said. "How are we going to discover Paige's cause of death?"

"Couldn't you ask Ian to reach out to the Rock Hill Police Department?" Mary asked Tina.

"My son hates it when I get involved in his Greensboro cases. He's not going to help me with a case in South Carolina."

"Mya, what about Todd?" Deniece asked.

She shook her head. "No way."

"Please." Tina made droopy, sad eyes.

"We aren't close," Myaisha said, avoiding a doubtful look on Deniece's face.

Tina begged with folded hands. "I'll owe you one."

"Two. You still owe me from the Christmas case."

"Okay. Two." Tina smiled eagerly. "I'll make your favorite Filipino dishes for a month."

"One month?"

"Two months."

She considered. "Six."

"What?" Tina shouted. She settled into the chair as people glared. "Sorry."

"Well?" Myaisha inquired.

"We'll be square on both favors."

"I get to name the dishes."

"Fine, but you supply the meats."

They shook hands. "Deal."

"Okay." Deniece glanced over at Myaisha's list. "So, Mya will get the cause of death. If it's murder, we'll move on to question two."

"Motives," Mary said, pointing to number three on Myaisha's list.

"Tina will uncover the names of each Charleston writing group member present at the conference."

"Oh, and send us copies of those room pictures," Deniece said.

"Um, I'd rather not," Tina demurred, lowering her gaze.

Deniece frowned. "You don't trust us."

"It's..." Tina hesitated. "The police might question you, and this way you can honestly say you weren't involved with me searching the room."

Noticing Deniece was about to speak, under the table with her shoe, Myaisha tapped her friend's foot. "I do want to glance over the pictures, though."

"Here." Tina slid her cellphone across the table.

The server dropped the check on the table. Myaisha provided a credit card while the ladies paid their portion of the bill to her in cash.

While glancing through the photos, Myaisha asked Tina, "Did you notice any syringes in the room?"

Wrinkles zigzagged along Tina's forehead. "I don't remember any, but I didn't get a chance to go into the bathroom."

Deniece asked, "Why, Mya?"

"When Paige passed out, I noticed an AV fistula in her left antecubital."

"She had end-stage renal disease?" Deniece asked.

Tina shrugged. "There's nothing on her blog about any health concerns."

Mary stood. "Not everyone shares their entire life online."

"Ask the people in her writing group." Myaisha rose and started to walk away from the table, then returned. "Oops. Forgot my tote bag."

Deniece followed Mary. "Joyce should know."

Outside, the South Carolina sun beat down with a stillness that intensified the heat. They walked precipitately toward the hotel.

Coming up beside Tina, Myaisha said, "We're going to help you, but you can't stress about succeeding as a true crime writer."

Tina ignored the comment and bolted through the hotel entrance with Mary close behind.

Myaisha entered using the revolving door. Once inside the hotel, she walked over to the bathroom where Paige collapsed.

"Desperation leads to tunnel vision. Tina's blind to the situation."

Deniece's brow arched. "Which is?"

"A homicide means there's a murderer, possibly a visitor, but more likely a person attached to the conference."

She stared at the door, which loomed larger with each second.

For half a minute, Deniece stood by her side as people strode by. Then she said, "And if they killed Paige..."

Myaisha's chest tightened. "They'll kill again."

Chapter 15

Outside the bathroom, Myaisha reclined against the wall and looked at her cellphone. Its weight increased the longer she contemplated the upcoming conversation. "I don't want to call Todd about this case."

Deniece's brow arched.

"Fine. I'll do it." Myaisha pressed the saved number on her cellphone.

"Ooh." Deniece made kissing noises while puckering her lips. "Todd has a special button on your phone."

Myaisha pivoted away, giving Deniece her back.

Three rings preceded. "Hello."

"Todd. Hi. This is Myaisha."

"Good afternoon, Doc. To what do I owe this pleasure?"

The mirth in his voice made her smile. "How are things?"

"Stop procrastinating," Deniece warned.

"Well. But I have a premonition my day is about to change."

Deniece made tiny circles with a finger, directing her to hurry.

Todd said, "You either stumbled across another dead body and are reporting a homicide, or you're interested in a dead body and have questions."

"I don't only call you about murders."

"True."

The softening of this tone made Myaisha's shoulders relax.

"I'll start over. What can I do for you?"

"I need a favor. Fast."

Todd's laugh boomed from the cellphone. Myaisha blushed, knowing Deniece heard it.

Her eyes closed. "Hypocrite, right? But it's urgent."

"Uh-huh. Which of my homicides have you become fascinated with this time?"

In a concise manner, Myaisha explained their trip to Rock Hill and how she assisted Paige in the bathroom.

"Doesn't sound like murder to me," Todd said.

"We didn't think so either until two homicide detectives interrogated me about what occurred."

Time passed. Neither spoke.

"You still there?" she asked.

"Yeah, sorry. Ian needed my signature on a report." Todd cleared his throat. "So, a woman you barely know died after a bout of diarrhea. Now, you and the Greensboro Women of Color Writing Group sense a homicide a foot."

"Funny."

"Rock Hill is in South Carolina. Not in my jurisdiction and not in North Carolina."

"Isn't there such a thing as interagency cooperation?"

"To get an autopsy report for an annoying friend who cannot enjoy a writing conference without uncovering a murder?"

"Yes."

He laughed. "What's the detectives' names?"

"D, give him the names?"

Deniece accepted the cellphone from Myaisha. "Hello, Todd."

"Couldn't you two do something relaxing? Pedicure or a spa day?"

"Sexist. What about hunting or white-water rafting?"

"Myaisha, white-water rafting?" he countered. "The only thing y'all hunt are killers."

Deniece provided Todd with the names of the homicide detectives.

"Give the phone back to Myaisha."

She said, "We need the results ASAP."

"Look. I'll reach out and see what information I can get. But they are not going to give me an autopsy report."

She frowned. "How do you know?"

"Because I wouldn't if I were in their position."

"Try asking nicely," she proffered.

"I lack your charm."

"Do your best."

"And what do I receive in exchange for this endeavor?"

She paused, unsure about his suggestive tone. "What do you mean?"

"Are my efforts to be unrewarded?"

Was he flirting?

Myaisha had previously considered and rejected Todd having a romantic interest in her. For a moment, she considered what he would judge appropriate compensation. "Chocolate bundt cake."

He countered. "Chocolate caramel cake."

"Done."

"Weekly for a month."

"Seriously?" She chuckled. "You'll make yourself sick."

"And you fail to appreciate my infatuation with chocolate."

Myaisha signaled Deniece. "Deal."

"Call you back." Todd hung up.

"The report's coming."

Deniece grinned. "There's nothing Todd wouldn't do for you."

"Stop." Myaisha consulted the list from the restaurant.

"He could have said no."

"But he didn't."

"Nothing's too much for his darling Myaisha." Deniece fluttered her eyelids.

"Let's move on."

Myaisha entered the bathroom, eager to avoid the possible truth in Deniece's comment.

Would Todd do anything for me?

Inside the bathroom, she inspected the area where Paige collapsed. Dull, dingy tiles retained no evidence of Thursday's tragedy.

Once the last person left the bathroom, Deniece asked, "What do you expect to find?"

"Don't know." Myaisha went into the stall Paige used. "Returning to the scene sometimes helps."

The putrid scent from Paige's illness had been replaced with a pine-scented cleanser.

"She wasn't killed here, though."

For a few seconds, Myaisha gazed blankly at her friend.

Deniece waved a hand in front of Myaisha's face. "Earth to Mya. Anyone home?"

"You're right. Paige wasn't murdered here. This is where she finally succumbed."

They exited the bathroom.

"The detectives are mum, but it had to be poison," Deniece said, as they ambled around the lobby.

"Though advantageous for the killer, poison presents a unique problem for a detective."

"And without knowing the exact poison, how do we begin to solve the where?"

Myaisha and Deniece completed a lap around the lobby.

"Who, what, when, why, where?"

"Huh?" Deniece eyed Myaisha.

"Working through my process." She checked her cellphone. Nothing from Todd. "If we can't decide on where, let's consider the why."

"Paige had an attitude. Remember how she acted when I commented about the pearls?"

Myaisha nodded.

"Clearly, she meddled in other people's business, even Fiction Writers of America's business."

"Her tenacity resulted in homicide?"

Deniece shrugged. "It could be related to her personal life."

"Possible. But I..." Myaisha recalled a comment Wednesday evening on the rooftop deck. An ominous comment about Paige's death, which proved coincidental.

But who made it?

Chapter 16

People bustled around the hotel like it was New York City's Grand Central Terminal. More than once, someone bumped into Myaisha as she stood in the middle of the walkway.

Deniece pulled her aside. "Trampled by a horde of writers." "Focus or you're going to be the next victim."

"I was distracted." Myaisha tried to discern who had made the comment Wednesday night about Paige.

It had to be Vinson or Rohrshack. They were speaking with Paige before I heard the comment.

But she had hidden behind a pillar. There could have been someone nearby, secluded behind the gardenias and topiary. Several pillars lined the hotel rooftop.

Myaisha's cellphone rang. The screen read *Tina*. She placed the cellphone on speaker and lowered the volume. "Yes?"

"Mary and I located four members of the Palmetto Writers," Tina said. "We'll talk to them—"

"After the poetry seminar," Mary added.

"Meet up at dinner," Tina said before hanging up.

Myaisha dropped the cellphone into her purse and consulted a map of the conference. "I'd like to check out the bookstore."

"First." Deniece plucked the map from between Myaisha's fingers. "As you said, divide and conquer."

Deniece headed for the FWA registration desk. "Let's go hunting."

On the way, Myaisha said, "Last night, about dinner."

"What are you babbling about?"

"Isolating."

While waiting in line at registration, Deniece said, "I wanted to be alone. This whole writing conference thing isn't for me."

Myaisha studied Deniece's profile. "Why did you come?"

"To support my friends and get out of the house."

She swallowed. "If you and Barry are going through—"

"Don't." Deniece held up a flat palm. "Leave it alone."

For now.

Minutes later, a smiling volunteer asked, "How may I help you?"

"We're looking for Mrs. Rohrshack," Myaisha said.

The volunteer reviewed a computer screen. "There's a book publishing workshop in the Charles Bolden Junior Conference Room on the second floor. Mrs. Rohrshack is hosting the event."

"Thanks."

Outside the conference room, Myaisha and Deniece waited for the session to end. Like columns, they stood on opposite sides of the doors.

"When this is over, we're going to talk," Myaisha said.

"It's about time. You need help on relationships *and* fashion."

Myaisha spied the smirk on her friend's mouth. "You first, sister."

The conference room doors parted before Deniece could reply. They entered against the tide of people exiting.

At the head of the conference room, Mrs. Rohrshack stood near a lectern surrounded by dozens of people. Myaisha glanced at her watch and wheedled her way between attendees.

"Can we schedule a meeting?" a short, brown-haired woman asked.

"Of course," Mrs. Rohrshack said. "Contact Tisha Newson. She handles all organizational scheduling."

"Mrs. Rohrshack," Myaisha said. "We have several questions about how Fiction Writers of America selects the Platinum Pen Award recipient."

"Inside the complementary tote bags, you'll find the entire process detailed in the conference syllabus." Mrs. Rohrshack headed toward the exit. "Now, if you'll excuse me."

People dispersed. Myaisha and Deniece trotted to keep up with Mrs. Rohrshack's lengthy strides.

"It will only take a moment," Myaisha said, darting around people to keep abreast of the FWA vice president.

"I'm sure you understand how busy things are right now," Mrs. Rohrshack said without stopping. "Direct your inquiries to our website. Someone will respond within forty-eight hours."

Deniece shoved an attendee aside and jumped in front of Mrs. Rohrshack. "This is about Paige Goodson."

Because Mrs. Rohrshack stopped abruptly, Myaisha slid into her backside. However, Mrs. Rohrshack's eyes fixed on Deniece.

"Yes. Such a terrible tragedy. We... Fiction Writers of America will make an announcement. Offer our condolences to her family and friends."

Myaisha asked, "Will the meeting be rescheduled?"

Penciled eyebrows angled along Mrs. Rohrshack's slick forehead. "What meeting?"

"The one Paige arranged to discuss her concerns about the Platinum Pen Award selection process."

Mrs. Rohrshack's slightly upturned nose twitched. "There is no meeting."

Deniece asked, "Because Paige died or because Fiction Writers of America doesn't want to be open about their selection process?"

A few stragglers from the seminar paused to listen to their exchange.

"There was no meeting to discuss the Platinum Pen Award. Our process is clear and transparent, as anyone familiar with the organization knows." Straightening her back, Mrs. Rohrshack enunciated with a pedantic tone. She marched out of the room.

Racing after her, Deniece shouted, "So if someone claimed voting for the Platinum Pen Award was rigged, you would say they were lying."

The daggers Mrs. Rohrshack shot Deniece made Myaisha's skin itch. She stood beside her friend.

"All we want are answers," Myaisha said.

Before a crowd could gather, Mrs. Rohrshack stormed off.

Myaisha and Deniece took the stairs down to the first floor.

"She knows something," Deniece said, checking her cellphone.

"And she's afraid. But why?"

Chapter 17

A chorus of a sports anthem rang out as enthusiastic revelers exited the hotel. Meanwhile, Myaisha and Deniece made their way over to a bench near an outside window. The former rested her head against the wall.

"Anything?" Deniece asked.

Myaisha checked her cellphone for messages. "AJ sent a photo of Boomer and Zoey." She shared the photo of two Labradors racing around the yard.

Deniece rolled her eyes.

"If you meant Todd, he hasn't responded yet."

Crossing her legs, Deniece pulled out her own cellphone.

"Are you expecting a call from Barry?" Myaisha tried to peek at the screen.

"I am not." Deniece snapped the cellphone shut.

"Things could've gone better with Mrs. Rohrshack." Myaisha stretched and yawned. "We've lost the element of surprise."

"We don't have time for civility."

Myaisha's forehead puckered. "There's always time for decency."

"The writing conference ends Sunday. We have to determine if Paige was murdered. And if so, how and by whom in three days." Deniece dropped the cellphone into her purse. "Any suggestions, Ms. Manners?"

"A bit testy, aren't we?"

"We are craving a little bump and grind."

Myaisha flushed.

"Oh, I'm sorry. Did I embarrass your highness?"

Her jaw tensed. "Sex doesn't embarrass me."

"Was it the bump and grind?"

"Crude."

"Prude."

She glared at Deniece.

"I thought you wanted to talk."

"Anyway." Myaisha took a deep breath before changing topics. "This is our first time at the Fiction Writers of America Conference. We don't know anyone in administration. We aren't familiar with their procedures."

"Has it ever stopped us before?" Deniece grinned. "We'll use more Southern hospitality."

"You don't like Mrs. Rohrshack, do you?"

"Mock our customs at your peril."

A chime on her watch alerted Myaisha to the hour. "Want to catch up with Tina and Mary?"

"It's not dinner time." Deniece rose.

"They might've learned something useful. Guide us to our next steps."

"Fine."

The phone dangled in Myaisha's hand as she glanced toward the hotel entrance. "Uh oh."

Deniece followed Myaisha's gaze. "What?"

"Police."

"Did that heifer call the cops on us?"

"Homicide."

Deniece followed Myaisha's gaze, then grabbed her hand.

"Where are we going?"

"To speak with them." Deniece hauled her across the hotel lobby.

Myaisha wrestled her hand free. "Are you crazy? If we get in trouble, how can we investigate?"

"We didn't do anything wrong." Deniece adjusted her blouse and checked her hair in a nearby glass case. "Besides, we can schmooze information out of them."

"No way."

"Use your magic, like you do on Todd."

Myaisha bristled. "I don't schmooze Todd."

"Flirt, simper. Do your thing."

She grabbed Deniece's arm. "I don't flirt with Todd. I'm involved with AJ."

"Are you trying to convince me or yourself?"

Before she could reply, the detectives approached.

"Dr. Douglas. Mrs. Withers." Detective Cambell gave a slight nod.

Deniece grinned. "So I'm included this time."

"Absolutely. Now I know we have two amateur sleuths in town," Detective Salter said.

Myaisha's jaw dropped.

Detective Cambell scratched his head. "Which is Easy Rawlins, and which is the murderous mouse?"

"I'm the murderous Mouse, with a capital M. Thank you." Deniece radiated pride.

Detective Salter laughed. "Gamble said you two were crazy."

Myaisha's shoulders tensed. "Todd, I mean Detective Gamble, spoke with you?"

"Don't worry," Detective Salter said. "Gamble suggested we collaborate. It's the surest way to get rid of the two of you."

"Where are the rest of the gang?" Detective Cambell surveyed the area.

Myaisha took a step forward. "It's only us."

"Um hmm." Detective Salter folded his arms over his chest.

"Todd also said the two of you have good insight," Detective Cambell added.

"We simply want answers," Myaisha said.

"Even when no one posed a question." Detective Salter directed them to the same alcove as before.

Away from hotel traffic, Detective Cambell said, "I would hope a doctor had enough to do besides getting involved in homicide investigations."

"She does this for kicks," Deniece said, avoiding Myaisha eye-balling her.

"Not true."

"I can't show you the autopsy report," Detective Salter said, removing a manila envelope from his suit coat pocket. "But I jotted down some findings the coroner shared."

Myaisha accepted the envelope. "Is the coroner an MD?"

"No, but when the blood samples returned, we sent the body—excuse me, Mrs. Goodson—to a forensic pathologist in Columbia."

While Myaisha skimmed the notes, Deniece asked, "Are blood samples routine?"

Detective Salter shook his head. "The ER doctor became suspicious when Mrs. Goodson coded. They transferred her to ICU, where she died the following morning."

While skimming the notes, Myaisha's eyes ballooned. Under her breath, she said, "Arsenic."

"This isn't proper procedure," Detective Cambell said. "And it better not come back to bite us in the ass." He removed sunglasses from his jacket pocket. "I'll be in the car."

A moment elapsed as they watched him depart.

Deniece read the notes over Myaisha's shoulder. "Someone poisoned Paige with arsenic."

"The ICU doctors must have done a spot urine test."

Deniece asked the detective, "Is homicide waiting for confirmation?"

Detective Salter didn't respond.

Myaisha said, "Arsenic can cause a rice water, cholera-type diarrhea. I remember smelling something on Paige's breath, but I couldn't swear it was garlic."

She folded the paper and secured it in her purse. "Thank you for this. I know it's hard to believe, but we aren't out to profit from this information."

"What about Mrs. de Jesus? She's a true crime author, correct?"

Myaisha and Deniece exchanged a quick glance.

Detective Salter's chin lifted. "Gamble and I go way back."

"Do you know Ian?"

"His partner?" The detective shook his head. "Gamble and I never worked together."

After a short scrutiny of the detective, Myaisha said, "Ex-military."

"I'm in the National Guard. Former active duty."

"You knew his sister."

"Gamble was right. You are sharp."

A softening in the detective's eyes recalled to Myaisha the tragedy which befell Todd's sister. "I'm sorry for your loss."

"She was a beautiful person." He looked away.

A moment of reflection passed before Deniece asked, "Can you tell us anything else?"

"Bold, brash, and easy on the eyes."

"Is that how Todd described me?" Deniece asked, her eyes sparkling.

The detective addressed Myaisha. "Give and take. Your turn."

"Right." Myaisha shared what they knew about Paige's suspicions about the Platinum Pen Award.

Detective Salter reclined against the wall. "People don't kill for writing contests."

"People kill for whatever reason they want. Often without one."

"This isn't some measly prize," Deniece said. "The winner receives ten thousand dollars and more in publicity."

"For an author, it can significantly boost their income and profile," Myaisha added.

"And this is on Mrs. Goodson's blog?" he asked.

They nodded.

"Why kill her if it's public knowledge?"

"When was the last time you read someone's blog?" Deniece asked.

Detective Salter shrugged. "Never."

"It's on the web, but not widely viewed outside the Palmetto Writers group or the Charleston writing community."

"And it simply referenced suspicions," Myaisha said.

"Paige didn't provide specifics," Deniece added.

The homicide detective's gaze bounced back and forth between them.

"Before this conference," Myaisha said, "Paige had arranged to meet with the Fiction Writers of America president. From what I overheard Wednesday night, they were going to discuss the award selection process, which Paige believed had been corrupted."

The detective removed a notepad from his suit coat pocket. "Name?"

Deniece removed a program syllabus from the tote and handed it to the detective. "Mya and I confronted Mrs. Rohrshack about the scheduled meeting, and she became livid."

Detective Salter's jaw clenched. "Ladies, don't stick your necks out. We aren't sure this is murder. But if a homicide was committed, this could be dangerous. If a person—"

"Killed once, they will kill again," Myaisha and Deniece repeated simultaneously with the detective.

He wiped his brow. "Gamble said y'all were determined—and nuts."

"We'll be careful," Myaisha said, "and keep you informed."

The detective snapped his notepad closed and replaced it in his coat pocket. He came within inches of Myaisha and Deniece. "Right now, this isn't an official homicide investigation. We're waiting for conclusive toxicology results. Once it *is* declared official, you two step aside."

As Deniece opened her mouth, Myaisha stepped on her foot. "Understood, Detective. And thank you again."

He held their gazes a second longer, then departed.

Once he was out of earshot, Deniece asked, "Why did you lie to him? We're not giving up."

"I said I understood, not that I agreed."

They bumped fists and headed for the elevators.

"We have the weapon," Deniece said.

Inside the elevator, Myaisha pressed button eleven. "Next is the who, how, and why."

"There's a conference full of suspects."

"Time to wheedle down the list." She inhaled. "And hope we don't face down another murderer."

Chapter 18

Elevator doors squeaked open, depositing them on the eleventh floor.

"They need to fix that," Myaisha said. "Rusted elevator doors do not inspire confidence in their reliability."

"I like this hotel—except the food."

"It's nice how they titled the conference rooms after South Carolina icons."

While Deniece fumbled for the door key card, Myaisha said, "We need to get something to eat before it gets late."

"We'll order room service."

"A minute ago, didn't you complain about the terrible food?"

"Oh, right."

Myaisha touched Deniece's arm. "Wait a minute. You didn't have dinner with us Wednesday or Thursday night."

"Nope."

"Did you order room service?"

Deniece swiped the card across the reader. "I ordered from an outside restaurant." She entered with Myaisha on her heels.

"From where?"

"There y'all are," Tina said, rising. "We have a guest."

Without answering Myaisha's question, Deniece approached the delicate woman standing beside Tina. "Nice to meet you."

Myaisha took a seat across the table while Tina made introductions.

"Alice is Paige's sister."

Without a DNA test, Myaisha refused to believe Paige and Alice were related. The women shared no similar features. Alice resembled a mythological nymph with her ballerina figure and straight, thin hair. She spoke with none of the regal command Paige exhibited the night before her death.

"Please accept our condolences," Myaisha said, studying the younger woman.

"Thank you." Alice's hand trembled as she reached for a glass of water. "It's nice to meet people who cared about Paige."

A scar in Alice's antecubital area triggered a memory. "You're on dialysis?" Myaisha asked.

"I was." Alice stuttered. "How did you know?"

Demonstrating on her own arm, Myaisha said, "The arteriovenous fistula."

Tina said, "Myaisha's a doctor."

Alice smiled sheepishly. "I received a kidney transplant last year."

"From Paige."

Tears rained down Alice's face and neck as she nodded. "She was an awesome sister."

Mary hugged Alice to her side as the latter sobbed.

"I'll be back." Deniece departed.

Myaisha watched her slip into the bedroom. Concern for Deniece would have to wait. Inching forward, she said, "We appreciate how hard this is for you."

"It doesn't matter. I can cry later." Alice wiped her face with a tissue Mary provided. "I want to know what happened to my sister."

"We don't know," Myaisha said, glancing at Tina and Mary.

"But." Alice dithered. "Tina promised you would find the truth."

Myaisha shot Tina a glare.

"I promised we would do our best to find out what happened," Tina clarified.

Mentally, Myaisha revised her to-do list to include talking with Deniece *and* Tina. Though she appreciated Tina's desire for a second career outside of medicine, Myaisha worried her friend was taking liberties.

What if we can't solve the crime?

Three days in a hotel with people they had no relationship with didn't bode well for their investigation.

Put it aside. Deal with Tina later.

"What was Paige like?" Myaisha asked.

Alice's face brightened. "Brilliant. Paige completed three years of undergraduate school before earning a master's degree in business.

After graduate school, she worked for a publisher in New York, which led her into books."

"I didn't know she had a business degree," Mary said.

Tina slid forward on her chair. "Paige shared her experiences in publishing with other authors."

"My sister bought and managed a bookstore," Alice continued. "She sold it for a profit before pursuing writing."

"I've read Paige's literary fiction books," Tina said, "but I believe she also wrote self-help books about the publishing industry."

"They aren't profitable like romance, but Paige believed they were more respectable—and what she knew best."

"General fiction is also more popular with writing award committees," Tina said with a tiny bit of forlornness in her voice.

Myaisha gave Tina a pointed glance before asking, "Alice, did you drive up here alone?"

Mary placed a hand on Alice's shoulder. "Any family or friends come with you?"

"Our parents died years ago. We don't have any family in South Carolina." Alice laughed lightly. "I'm sure you noticed the differences in our ages."

They nodded.

"Momma had Paige as a teenager and me at menopause. We have different fathers."

Perfect explanation for the differences in their appearances.

In a sensitive tone, Myaisha said, "Paige was a second mother to you."

Alice agreed, sending another flurry of tears streaming down her face. Mary provided tissues. Tina rubbed her back.

In a choked voice, Alice said, "It's why I'm determined to find out what happened. Paige deserves justice."

Tina avoided Myaisha's gaze. "We want to help."

A barely audible "Thank you" came from the weeping sister.

Myaisha asked, "How did you guys meet?"

"In the hotel lobby. I recognized Alice from Paige's blog." Tina addressed Alice, "She was very proud of you."

"What brought you to the hotel?" Myaisha asked.

"The police contacted me this morning, and I drove up right away." Alice stifled a sob. "The hotel gave Joyce a new room. I wanted to retrieve Paige's personal items before they were confiscated."

Alice sat up and blew her nose. "It makes me angrier than sin. Someone stole from my sister while she was dying in the hospital."

Myaisha's brows rose.

The detectives hadn't mentioned any theft.

"I don't understand."

Tina said, "There's a book missing from Paige's luggage."

"A rare book," Alice added. "Paige sold the store but continued to secure rare books for particular clients."

The word particular piqued Myaisha's interest. "Particular how?"

"Wealthy," Mary said.

"More like influential." With a mirror, Alice checked her splotchy face. "I apologize for making a scene."

"Understandable," Mary said.

"It was only you and Paige," Tina said.

"We had each other. Nothing else mattered," Alice said.

"Would these *particular* people hurt your sister?" Myaisha asked.

"Why would they? Paige took a nominal commission and dealt fairly with customers."

Tiny, studded pearl earrings dotted Alice's earlobes. A designer bag rested beside her legs. Clearly, the sisters shared an interest in luxury goods.

Was it pertinent? Had Paige's expensive habits led to murder? Too many questions. I need more facts.

"Paige made a decent income," Myaisha said.

Alice's smile stretched from ear to ear. "My sister was rich. Our parents worked hard but gave us little. Paige earned every dime she made. She took care of our parents and me." Alice's chin quivered.

To ward off another crying spell, Myaisha said, "Tell us about the missing book."

Deftly, Alice removed a binder from her bag. She flipped around several pages before handing over a half dozen sheets of paper.

Myaisha read the top page. "*Antiquarium Botanique.*"

Tina peered over Myaisha's shoulder. "A book on botany?"

Alice stood as if to give a lecture. "Not any botany book, but one from the eighteenth century. Drawings with exquisite details. Prints of plants and animals created by different authors."

Alice kneeled next to Myaisha's chair, pointing out certain descriptions. "This collection of prints is bound in a unique cover, its edges dipped in gold. Special pigments creating vibrant, unique colors."

A memory tugged at the edge of Myaisha's brain. "Electric emerald green."

"Uh-hmm. A lovely color. Not to mention the drawings and pictographs." Alice spoke with animation. "This book is a one-of-a-kind classic work of art."

Myaisha fingered the drawings, reading the description of the collection and its provenance. "And if I recall, artisans used arsenic to develop those luscious colors."

Chapter 19

Myaisha tried to recall where she first read about arsenic-tainted books. It would be a nice reference at this moment. Instead, she asked, "Are you staying at the hotel?"

Alice rose. "My boyfriend is picking me up. We're staying in Rock Hill for the weekend. Until..." She sniffed.

Myaisha escorted her to the door. "I'll ride with you down to the lobby."

"Wait," Tina said. "We'll go too."

With a sideways glance, Myaisha regarded Tina, who maintained a neutral demeanor.

"Have you had a chance to speak with any members of Paige's writing group?" Myaisha asked.

"Not since I got to the hotel." Alice blew her nose. "Joyce called me after she heard about Paige."

"She didn't call when EMS took Paige to the hospital?" Myaisha asked.

Alice shook her head. "No, but..."

Myaisha and Tina observed the young lady expectantly.

"People in Paige's writing group knew about her kidney disease. This isn't the first time my sister had to be taken to the hospital."

"Oh," Myaisha and Tina said in unison.

"Paige passed out before. She'd get busy and forget to take her medication."

"Had she been ill before this trip?" Myaisha entered the elevator. "Passed out or lost consciousness in the past week."

A dimpling of Alice's brow signaled she considered the question. "The last time we spoke, Paige hadn't mentioned anything serious. She'd been tired, but nothing significant."

The elevator opened, and they exited the cabin.

Alice proceeded them into the hotel lobby. "I don't expect to hear from any members of Palmetto Writers, especially not—"

"There you are." Joyce approached, embracing Alice in a bear hug. "Poor child. How are you holding up?"

Myaisha observed the exchange between the women. Alice's arms remained unenthusiastically at her sides.

"I've been so concerned about you." The older woman's hawkish nose twitched. "Did you drive up from Charleston alone?"

Joyce wore no makeup, except lip gloss, and her black, graying hair formed a tight bun on the top of her head. Sensible shoes, slacks, and a blouse. Nothing fashionable about Joyce, not even a handbag. She carried the FWA complimentary tote bag, which brimmed with books and miscellany.

"You've been busy," Myaisha said, pointing at the tote bag.

In an aside to Alice, Joyce said, "Please forgive me, dear. I did attend several programs today, not that your sister's passing hasn't upset me."

"I understand," Alice said. "This is your one big trip each year."

Pivoting toward Myaisha, Joyce said, "A librarian doesn't get many opportunities to travel."

"Unsung heroes of the public information system," Myaisha said, straining to identify the items in Joyce's tote bag.

"Since you're meeting up with someone, I'll be off." Joyce started to depart.

"Perhaps we could speak later," Myaisha inquired, "when you have a moment."

"Unlikely. I have events scheduled way into Sunday afternoon." Joyce hurried away.

"I'm sure something can be arranged," Myaisha called after the departing librarian.

"She was in a hurry," Tina said.

Myaisha watched Joyce's retreat. "To an event or to sanctuary."

"She's always been odd." Alice moved toward the hotel's entrance. "Paige felt sorry for her."

In answer to Myaisha's widened gaze, Alice said, "Librarians make little money, and Joyce loves to travel. She accompanied Paige on book-buying expeditions—at my sister's expense, of course."

Recalling the brief conversation they had shared, Myaisha said, "Paige was a kind person. I wish I had known her better."

Though the lapse in conversation was brief, it hinted at an unspoken element. About Paige's character? She gazed at Alice, puzzled.

Whether from Myaisha's perusal or another emotion, Alice flushed. "Yes, well…"

Tina said, "I'm sure she meant the generosity kindly."

A secret understanding seemed to pass between Tina and Alice.

"It wasn't always understood." Alice stared out of the hotel's immense windows. "People resented Paige's help. They accepted it but scorned her for being superior."

Myaisha fumbled to find the correct words to elicit more information. "Money can make friendships awkward."

Alice swung around sharply, glaring at Myaisha. "I warned her. Paige associated with anyone, with no regard for their financial circumstances." Alice observed them as if prepared to meet a challenge.

"She liked to share," Tina said.

Myaisha wondered if her friend truly believed that or if she stated it to garner further exposition.

"Paige was successful. Her less affluent friends accepted her generosity, but they called her bourgeois. Mocked her for being arrogant."

The waif's features hardened. "My sister worked hard. Paige could afford nice things and treated herself well. If she wanted company, she paid for everything—travel, food, and shopping."

"Kindness is often resented," Myaisha said, tactfully avoiding assumptions.

"So unfair. They never appreciated Paige." Tears flooded Alice's eyes. "I hate the entire Palmetto Writers group."

In a flurry, Alice stormed outside.

"I'll go after her," Myaisha said. "Make sure she's okay."

"There's an author roundtable in the Marian Wright Edelman Conference Room," Mary said, viewing the program schedule. "Talk later." She dashed off.

Tina said, "I want to talk with Rhonda and Tullulah, if I get a chance between all those fanatics."

"Let's regroup at dinner," Myaisha said before walking outside.

Under the hotel's shaded portico, Myaisha hugged a sobbing Alice to her side.

Minutes passed before she said, "I don't want to appear uncaring, but I need to ask about the Charleston writing group. Paige voiced concerns about the Fiction Writers of America Platinum Pen Award. Did she discuss this with you?"

Alice shook her head and wiped tears away with the back of her hand. "I'm not into books."

They watched traffic on the street in front of the hotel.

Myaisha checked her watch. Thoughts coalesced in her mind. "Paige developed renal failure after donating her kidney," she stated more than asked.

"Ironic and cruel." Alice searched inside her purse. "Where's my cellphone? Tad should be here by now."

How can I get information without sharing the detectives' suspicions about arsenic? The direct approach would be easier.

"Anything else you remember about Paige's illness before she left Charleston?"

"Not much." Alice frowned. "She mentioned some bad food she ate over the weekend. It started after her birthday party. We celebrated at a seafood restaurant in downtown Charleston."

Seafood would support food poisoning, not arsenic.

Alice watched the horizon, speaking indifferently. "People brought gifts. We had dinner and champagne. The next day, Paige felt fatigued, but she had received dialysis."

"Dialysis is exhausting."

"It left Paige drained. But she also drank a lot of champagne the night before–for her birthday."

"Rough on the one kidney."

Alice's chin trembled. "This is my fault. She'd been in perfect health before donating her kidney."

Myaisha laid a hand on Alice's shoulder. "It may seem that way, but renal transplantation is safe. The onset of Paige's renal disease was simply coincidental."

"I wish I could believe you."

"It's true. Your donated kidney is working fine, right?"

"Paige should be alive. If not for her donation, I would be dead, not her."

Myaisha yearned to explain Paige died from arsenic, not because of a renal disease, but Detective Salter swore her to secrecy. Besides, arsenic as a cause of Paige's death had not been confirmed. In addition, there was the existence of a rare, valuable book possibly tainted with arsenic, which conveniently disappeared. The book might be the source of Paige's arsenic poisoning.

"I need to understand why Paige died so suddenly." Alice chewed on her bottom lip.

"Did any specific person in Palmetto Writers resent Paige? Not her business success, but from a writing perspective?"

"Resent?" Alice's voice faltered as if she considered the word. "I loved my sister, but her writing was basic."

"I can relate. It's difficult to write original, dynamic prose, especially with so much competition."

"Paige easily secured an agent from her New York contacts. But her book sales were lukewarm."

How can I ask about the FWA without raising Alice's suspicions?
"Did Paige fear anyone?"

"Hardly." Alice giggled. "My sister feared no one or anything."
"I see."

Alice lifted her chin. "Paige had no tolerance for idiots or cheaters."

Myaisha's brow lifted. "Had she encountered dishonesty in her writing group?"

Because Alice stepped away, Myaisha believed she'd pushed too hard, too fast.

"Why do you ask?"

"Have you read Paige's website?"

"Writing doesn't interest me." Alice sized Myaisha up as if seeing her for the first time. "What's on it?"

"Your sister suspected dishonesty in the Fiction Writers of America Platinum Pen Award contest." Myaisha hesitated to mention Paige's interaction with Tullulah.

"Did she?" Alice's gaze narrowed. "Why are you asking me these questions?"

"I—"

"My sister is dead, and you're asking me about some stupid writing contest?"

"Right." Myaisha backed down, not wanting to destroy their burgeoning relationship. She might need Alice later. "I apologize. Paige should be remembered beyond this writing group."

A heaviness hung between the women. Perspiration dripped down Myaisha's back. She ached to return to the air-conditioned hotel but needed to maintain a cordial rapport. The addition of this rare book added a new dimension to Paige's death, with Alice as her sole access.

They stood side by side as a yellow sedan drove up to the curb. The driver waved as Alice headed for the car.

Myaisha said, "Unfortunately, I didn't know Paige long." She handed Alice a card. "If I can do anything for you, let me know."

Alice read the card. "Dr. Douglas. You're a medical doctor."

"Yes, but I didn't treat your sister. We met because of our mutual writing interests."

With a slight nod, Alice slipped into the sedan, which swiftly drove off. A beat later, Myaisha bolted inside the hotel.

Myaisha considered what she had learned. Little to explain Paige's death—or murder. In fact, the rare book complicated matters. Her shoulders slumped.

"Perhaps I should focus on Fiction Writers of America. It's the reason we came here."

Even as she walked across the lobby, Myaisha knew she wouldn't stop investigating. Paige died—or was murdered—conveniently before a scheduled meeting with the FWA president. Coincidence?

Poisoning could be done from a distance. Paige's killer didn't have to be present at the writing conference.

But how was the arsenic delivered?

If the murderer wasn't at the conference, they had to be sure of their delivery mechanism. Did Paige have to die before she could meet with the FWA president? If the poisoning originated in Charleston, the Platinum Pen Award might have had no connection with the poisoning.

There could be other motives for Paige's death. For instance, Alice would likely inherit as the sole living relative.

Don't fall for the innocent loving sister ploy. Alice is no fool.

When the police informed her of Paige's death, Alice immediately headed for the hotel and this rare, valuable book.

Might be reflex. Might be murder.

"D was right. Solving mysteries had become a drug."

As a physician, Myaisha understood the dangers of addiction.

Chapter 20

A figure rapidly approached Myaisha's vicinity. In addition to the vivid orange lipstick, Myaisha easily identified Rhonda from her platinum blond hair. She made a beeline for the Charlestonian.

"Mrs…" She didn't know Rhonda's last name. "Excuse me. Do you have a moment?"

Rhonda side-glanced at Myaisha without slowing down. "I thought it would be obvious by my speed. I do not." A silver bracelet with miniature trinkets jingled around Rhonda's porcelain wrist.

She must avoid sunlight. Vampires have more blemishes than she does.

Huffing, Myaisha increased her gait. "You could make a speed walker blush."

"Well, I believe in staying in shape."

The appraisal from Rhonda made Myaisha bristle.

"It will only take a moment."

"Time I do not have." Rhonda rounded the corner and descended a wide staircase.

"This concerns Paige Goodson, a member of Palmetto Writers."

"I'm preoccupied with our breathing members." Rhonda's abrupt stop caused Myaisha to hop down a step to avoid a collision.

"Look, Tullulah has a dozen demands, half of which I would like to complete this afternoon."

"You work for Tullulah?"

I... Not specifically," Rhonda hesitated. "I'm an editor. So, I assist authors with manuscripts, query letters, synopses. My client list is substantial."

Circling around Myaisha, she said, "There are more productive things to do at this conference than meddling in the death of a stranger. Unless you're one of those true crime weirdos."

Addressing Rhonda's back, she said, "Paige was a friend."

In a dismissive wave, Rhonda said, "Leave it to the police."

At a pace Myaisha failed to match, Rhonda sprinted into a conference room.

"I need to get in shape. Maybe AJ lost interest because of my expanding waistline."

Myaisha rested on a bench and dabbed her sweaty forehead with a tissue.

"I've always been a big girl. It must be something else. He's very fit. I could participate in more physical activities with him."

Once her heart rate moderated, Myaisha climbed the staircase to the hotel lobby floor. Rhonda hadn't been the first person to tell her to leave things to the police.

"I didn't take their advice, and I'm definitely not listening to Rhonda."

At a slower pace, Myaisha climbed the steps to the lobby floor.

"Wait a minute." She rested against the handrail. Something she'd heard had been significant. But what?

Alice. Rhonda. It could've been Tina or Mary, for all she knew.

She smacked the rail and immediately regretted it. Myaisha replayed the day's conversations. An important nugget sat in the recesses of her mind. At a snail's pace, she pondered what she had missed and how it pertained to Paige's death.

"Hello."

Myaisha flinched at the tap on her shoulder.

"Oh, sorry." The woman retreated a step. "Didn't mean to startle you."

"Can I help you?"

"Hope so."

A ball cap sporting the state baseball team sat low across the woman's forehead. Two foot-long braids draped across her shoulders. Light green, thick-rimmed frames perched on a boxy nose. Myaisha could barely view the woman's blue eyes.

"Do I know you?"

A left-side grin crept across the woman's lip. "Are you a true crime reader?"

"Afraid not."

The grin faded. "Figures."

"Pardon me?"

"Forget it." The woman guided Myaisha off to the side, away from bystanders. "I was in the conference room when the police asked for the person who assisted Paige in the bathroom."

Myaisha frowned, determined not to disclose anything the Rock Hill detectives shared about Paige's death. "Go on."

"I was also there when you and your friend confronted Betty."

"Who are you?"

"Sorry." The woman slipped a book out of her tote bag. "Lynn Wren."

Accepting the book, Myaisha read the cover and inside jacket. "This is your book?"

"Not bad, right?"

"Quite nice." Myaisha returned it. "So, what can I do for you?"

"Paige's death." Lynn cozied up to her. "It wasn't natural, was it?"

"Why do you say that?"

Lynn chuckled. "Two police detectives questioning a participant in a writers conference about a woman who died suddenly in a bathroom. Not any woman. A woman who suspected the Fiction Writers of America's award contest was rigged."

Myaisha's left brow arched. "You read Paige's blog?"

"After she died." Lynn shook her head. "Who still blogs?"

"A sudden death at a writers conference. How does that concern me—or you?"

"Cut me in."

"What—"

"To the murder investigation."

"I'm not sure what you believe is going on."

"Nice try, but I have a contact in the Rock Hill Police Department. I know they have opened a murder investigation."

"Then you know more than I do." Myaisha started to leave.

"Perhaps I do." Lynn laid a hand on her arm. "Ask de Jesus if she wants to collaborate. I have an in with the Palmetto Writers."

Myaisha accepted the card Lynn proffered without responding. It listed Lynn's name, books, and contact information.

"Think about it."

One of the conference room doors opened, and people streamed by. Myaisha weighed whether to discuss Lynn's proposal with Tina or to throw the card in the trash.

"I better tell her. Lynn might approach Tina on her own."

Myaisha dropped the card in her tote bag, worried a competitive Tina might be worse than a murderous poisoner.

Chapter 21

Disinterested in any of the evening's programs, Myaisha wandered aimlessly around the lobby. Neither Tina nor Mary cared to meet up for dinner.

Tina wanted to work on a new manuscript, and Mary stumbled across a group of poets who'd scheduled an impromptu reading. Deniece hadn't responded to any calls or texts. Myaisha had the evening to herself.

Who should I talk to next? Who had a motive to kill Paige?

If the poisoning originated in Charleston, Paige's concerns about Platinum Pen were immaterial to her murder. Paige's attendance at the conference could be coincidental.

"Multiple coincidences?" Myaisha shook her head. "One, maybe. But Paige's poisoning, the theft of a book laced with arsenic, and suspicions about a writing award. These instances must be related."

Questions percolated around her mind as she spotted Hunter Vinson. The chairperson of the membership committee strolled down the lobby with two other people. Myaisha hustled over to them.

"Mr. Vinson?"

He gave a commercial-worthy smile. "Hello."

"This is my first conference. My Greensboro, North Carolina, writing group is considering joining."

"Excellent. How can I help?" He excused himself from the other people. "I'll join you in a moment."

Once his companions departed, he faced Myaisha. "Did you need help with registration? The website has a section for group memberships. Instructions—"

"Were you able to meet with Paige before she died?"

Vinson blanched.

Aware of her blunt approach, Myaisha had sacrificed grace for time. "Forgive my lack of decorum, but I appreciate your busy schedule."

He swallowed visibly, scanning the area as if seeking assistance. "I..." His bony Adam's apple bobbed inside his reedy neck.

"On her blog, Paige questioned the legitimacy of the Platinum Pen Award. She suspected duplicity in the selection process. Though she didn't mention Tullulah Bishop by name, she alluded to a member of the Charleston writing group repeatedly winning the award."

Vinson wiped sweaty hands on his slacks. "Perhaps, but I had no idea about Mrs. Goodson's concerns. She hadn't mentioned any suspicions to me."

"I heard her address you and Mrs. Rohrshack Wednesday night at the rooftop bar. Yesterday, Paige had a scheduled meeting with the Fiction Writers of America president, who is noticeably absent."

"How?" His eyes enlarging, Vinson stammered. "When did you hear us?"

"The night before Paige died."

His jaw clenched. "I'm not sure what you believe you overheard, but I assure you, we discussed nothing untoward regarding the Platinum Pen Award process."

Myaisha sighed. "Don't make me work to get the information."

Vinson squared his shoulders. "Excuse me. I have duties to attend to."

"When the truth comes out, you'll want to be on the side of the angels," Myaisha said, addressing his back.

He pivoted around and glowered at her before storming away.

"Great job." She lifted the tote onto her shoulder. "Making friends everywhere. At this rate, the Greensboro Women of Color Writing Group will be barred from joining Fiction Writers of America."

Grumbles from her stomach made Myaisha head for the bar. At nine in the evening, one restaurant remained open, and she had tried their fare before.

"A bar should at least have nachos or sliders. Anything had to be better than the hotel restaurant's food."

At the bar entrance, Myaisha allowed her eyes to adjust to the low lighting. The room consisted of around fifteen tables, most occupied by couples. Across from the entrance, a burned wood-toned bar ran the entire length of the room with over two dozen stools. On the left, Myaisha spied a vacant seat close to the kitchen. Like a bird of prey, she swooped down and hopped on the stool.

A cheery bartender asked, "What can I get you?"

"A menu, please."

"The menu is only available to bar customers."

She huffed. "I'll have a daiquiri."

"Coming up," he said, sliding a menu across the Corian countertop.

Though not a teetotaler, Myaisha didn't want to imbibe. She needed to puzzle out the mystery surrounding Paige's death. She ordered fries and cheeseburger sliders. Swiveling on the stool, she scanned the restaurant.

People watching helped her create story ideas and craft plots. She might notice a person reading a book and imagine they were an undercover operative on assignment. A woman pushing a stroller might be an assassin carrying an assortment of guns instead of a baby.

Ideas came from ordinary events. An overheard conversation might give her a new character name. She studied people's faces, trying to uncover their secrets, passions, and fears from their expressions or mannerisms.

Those activities hadn't helped her finish any books, though. Myaisha believed her stories lacked a certain *je ne sais quoi*. Unable to identify their deficits, she couldn't complete those stories. Manuscripts piled up. Over the years, her dream of publishing diminished.

"May I have a Manhattan?"

Two stools down, Myaisha noticed a swaggering Tisha Newson slog up to the bar. Cognizant of the award committee chairwoman's intoxicated state, Myaisha figured it would be an opportune time for questions.

Nothing like liquor to loosen lips.

The bartender slid the drink over to Newson. "Should I charge it to your room?" he asked.

Myaisha plopped two bills on the countertop. "I got it."

He palmed the bills, and Newson gave Myaisha a glossy-eyed perusal.

"Do we know each other?" Newson's brows knitted in an apparent effort of concentration.

"You probably saw me around the hotel." Myaisha slid her food over to sit beside Newson. "Consider it a token of appreciation for the volunteer work you do."

Newson laughed, sloshing a bit of liquid onto the bar. "Volunteer. You must be drunk."

The pot is calling the kettle black.

"I'm paid for my work," Newson asserted, winking knowingly at Myaisha.

"As well you should be. It can't be easy coordinating the award ceremony. Arranging the books and judges."

"Horrible." Newson swallowed half the glass. "This is my last year unless things change."

Stealthily, Myaisha slid closer. She noticed the bartender eyeing Newson, and her voice lowered. "I don't understand. What needs to change?"

"Don't tell anyone." With a wobbling finger, Newson motioned Myaisha closer. "The secret to successful publishing isn't writing." Her head shook unsteadily. "Editing. Classes. Marketing. Tons of money in publishing, just not in writing books."

A spray of alcoholic spittle sprinkled Myaisha. Discreetly, she wiped her face. "You're an editor?"

"Nope." Newson sipped her drink. "I conduct classes on publishing, writing, marketing."

"Have you written any books?"

"On how to write." Tisha gave Myaisha a suggestive grin. "Don't write novels myself, but tell other people how to do it. Tons of money in publishing."

With a guffaw, she slapped the countertop. "Writers are suckers. They'll pay anything to get published. Or see their novel in their town bookstore. These idiots believe they're gonna be the next Nora Roberts."

Though interested in the topic, Myaisha needed information before Newson passed out drunk or got kicked out.

"We were talking about the Platinum Pen Awards program. Remember?"

With a wave of her hand, Newson said, "It's over. I'm out."

Exasperated, Myaisha leaned closer. "Why? Tell me what's been going on."

In a higher tenor, Newson said, "Why you asking about the award process?" The award committee chair's glazed eyes squinted.

Like an eagle capturing its prey, the bartender swooped in and confiscated Tisha's glass. "You've had enough."

Newson's mouth opened as if to reply, but it remained silent and gaping. Without answering, she stumbled away.

Myaisha attempted to assist her, but Newson tussled free.

Back at the bar, Myaisha slurped her drink. At least Newson confirmed Paige's suspicions about something untoward occurring with the Platinum Pen Award process. But what?

Myaisha sprinkled extra salt on her fries and devoured her meal.

"Need anything?" the bartender asked.

She licked sauce off her lips. "These sliders are divine."

"Should I place another order? The kitchen closes at ten."

"Please." Myaisha wiped a drizzle of ketchup off her chin.

Couples entered and departed while she consumed her meal. The bartender refreshed her drink. In time, Paige and FWA drifted aside. Myaisha admired the couples nestled around the room.

When was the last time AJ and I went out to dinner?

He'd been occupied with his new business venture. Frustrated about the housing crash, AJ rehabilitated smaller affordable homes. Commercial contractors built larger houses for larger profits, he bemoaned. His homes would be for average working-class families. But with his current job as a firefighter, this meant he devoted downtime to renovation and construction. No time for romance.

Sadness weighed down Myaisha's chest. Or was it alcohol and grease?

A flirtatious couple in a corner booth made her smile. Despite their maturity, they bantered like teenagers, caressing and giggling. Myaisha was too far away to appreciate their words. But from their gaiety, it seemed like a safe assumption they were joking and teasing each other.

The man's bushy mustache and beard hid most of his face. She admired his cap, covering bushy dreadlocks. In a riotous laugh, the woman tossed her head, briefly pivoting in Myaisha's direction.

Daiquiri squirted out of her nose, as Myaisha choked.

The bartender rushed over. "Everything okay?"

Using the napkins he provided, Myaisha mopped liquor off her face. "May I have a glass of water?"

"Sure."

As the bartender retrieved a glass, Myaisha surreptitiously watched the couple.

"I can't believe it."

"Believe what?" The bartender handed her a glass.

"Oh, nothing." She sipped water. "I didn't realize I was talking out loud."

The bartender viewed her suspiciously.

He thinks I'm drunk.

"May I have those sliders to go?" she asked.

"One minute." He looked as if he would be glad to see her leave.

Once he departed, Myaisha returned to watching the couple. She needed to confirm what she thought she saw.

The man rose and tipped his cap at the woman. Not any woman. It was Deniece.

Her best friend—married best friend—was dining with a man who was not her husband.

"What am I going to do?"

"About what?" The bartender had returned without her noticing.

She ignored his question and asked for the bill.

"What room are you in?" he asked. "I'll put it on the tab."

"I prefer to pay cash."

He set the bill on the countertop. Myaisha dropped several twenties and a ten.

"Keep the rest."

"Appreciate it. Sure you're all right?" he asked, scooping up the money with a roguish lilt to his lips. "I can escort you to your room."

Under six feet with dark, lanky hair pulled back in a ponytail, the bartender was not her type.

Not AJ.

"I'm fine." To set his mind at ease, she said. "I'm a writer. Talking to myself is how I work out plots."

An inviting grin lit across his face. "Oh, yeah. I heard there's a writers conference going on. Have you published anything?"

"I wish."

Noticing Deniece and the man exiting, Myaisha thanked the bartender, slid her to-go tray into the tote bag, and left.

She stopped precipitously beside a miniature palmetto tree adjacent to the bar. From between fronds, she watched Deniece and the bearded man. Lobby traffic prevented her from understanding their conversation, but she snatched pieces.

Two things stood out: Saturday night and room 812.

Chapter 22

Despite a late evening discussing Paige's sudden demise and allegations against FWA, Myaisha awoke before dawn. Last night, it took over an hour to calm Tina down about Lynn's intrusion into their investigation.

Myaisha planned to speak with several people, hopefully before the morning conference events commenced. She tiptoed into the bathroom, showered, and dressed. Once more, she tapped Deniece on the shoulder.

"Can we talk?" she whispered, not wanting to disturb Tina and Mary in the second bedroom.

"Hmm." Deniece mumbled and rolled over.

Myaisha shook her shoulders. "D wake up. We have to talk."

"What time is it?" Deniece mumbled with her eyes closed tight.

"Seven."

"In the morning. Are you insane?" Deniece rolled over, giving Myaisha her backside.

"It's important."

"Go away."

"Listen."

A pillow struck the wall beside Myaisha's head.

"Quiet. This is my vacation."

"We *are* going to talk."

"Not right now." Deniece crawled under the covers.

Myaisha departed, softly shutting the door.

In the common area of the suite, she found Tina typing at a desk near the window. A sliver of sunlight shone through the partially parted drapes.

"Morning."

"Hey." Tina's eyes stayed locked on the computer. "Why are you up so early?"

Myaisha heated water and dropped a tea bag into a mug. "There are people I need to speak with."

Tina stopped typing. "Who?"

She detailed her plans for the day.

"Sounds good. If I finish this chapter before the true crime workshop, I'll meet up with you."

"By the way, did you get the room numbers for any of the Charleston writing group members?" Myaisha asked, spooning sugar into the mug.

"Only Joyce and Rhonda." Tina handed Myaisha a writing pad. "No one else volunteered theirs, and I couldn't figure out how to ask without coming off like a stalker. This Lynn person must have warned them against me."

Myaisha jotted down the information and set the pad down on the desk. "Last night, you talked with Tallulah Bishop. What's your impression? Would she cheat to win an award?"

"It wasn't a social conversation. I was immersed in a crowd of her admirers." Tina stretched and leaned back in the chair. "What I do know is Tallulah has won the Platinum Pen Award more than any other author since the contest originated."

"But would she pay to win an award?"

Tina shrugged. "Couldn't tell. But she has done well professionally. Her books sell, and she is held in high esteem by other authors."

Myaisha stood. "Who are the judges?"

"I don't know. Check the website."

"Can I use your computer?" She scooted a chair up beside the desk.

In a few clicks, Tina brought up the website. Scrolling between pages, she eventually located the award page.

They frowned.

"They aren't listed," Tina said.

"Strange."

For a moment, they stared at the screen before again scanning the website.

"Not exactly transparent, but I'm not sure it's suspicious."

"Perhaps." Myaisha returned the chair to the dining area.

"Call me if you discover anything." Tina resumed typing.

"Are those notes for the new book?"

"Yep." Tina swatted a stray hair from her brow. "Want to get a synopsis down ASAP before the police make an official announcement. I'll shoot it over to my agent this morning."

Last night during her conversation with Tina and Mary, Myaisha hadn't shared Detective Salter's information concerning arsenic. In her zeal to meet the publisher's demands, Tina might use the information before the authorities confirmed Paige's death as an official homicide.

Should I inform the homicide detectives about the leak in their department?

It would require more thought.

Todd vouched for Myaisha, not Tina. Deniece knew about the arsenic, but she had other preoccupations. Was her best friend having an affair?

Myaisha couldn't believe it. Deniece and Barry seemed devoted to each other. Sure, they had experienced a difficult time and a divorce. But their breakup occurred over ten years ago. Other than their fertility problems, the couple appeared happily married.

Where did her loyalties lie? She loved them both. Deniece was like family. But she couldn't condone an illicit affair.

"No wonder she'd been irritable lately. Guilty conscience."

"Excuse me," Tina said. "I didn't hear what you said."

"Thinking out loud." Myaisha departed, determined to stop talking to herself, at least audibly.

As she headed for the elevators, Myaisha considered whom to tackle first. Whether Paige died from accidental or intentional poisoning, the Platinum Pen Award process needed investigating.

I hope my questions don't lead me to Paige's fate.

Chapter 23

Stationed in the hotel lobby beside a pillar, Myaisha observed employees and volunteers preparing for the conference's fourth day.

A multicolored table runner with the Fiction Writers of America insignia draped over two long tables ran perpendicular to the hotel's registration desk. The change in location probably indicated most participants had completed their conference registration.

Myaisha waited, stalking the vicinity of the tables. She had a list of people to speak with. The order didn't matter.

Seconds after the elevator pinged, a familiar face approached the volunteer table. Giving the woman a moment to settle down, Myaisha pounced.

She plastered on a dazzling smile and greeted the volunteers. "Good morning. Nice to see other early risers."

Several volunteers returned her greeting.

"It's Mrs. Newson, right?" Myaisha asked, already knowing the answer and assessing whether Newson remembered their brief tête-à-tête in the bar last night.

"Hello," Tisha Newson answered with a tight grin.

"I thought so." Myaisha amplified the charm. "On the website, it mentioned you chair the Platinum Pen Award committee."

"Uh, yes." A tiny hesitation crept into Newson's reply. "Guidelines and rules are posted on the website."

"They are, but I didn't find a list of the judges. Do you have one?"

Newson's gaze drifted from Myaisha to the volunteers. Because of the early hour and empty line, the volunteers' attention focused on their conversation.

"No problem." A blush formed across Newson's throat. "I can forward the information via email."

"I don't have my computer with me. As the chairperson, I'm sure you know their names off the top of your head."

Though Myaisha's gaze zeroed in on Newson, she appreciated the volunteers watching the committee chairwoman.

One of the volunteers said, "I had wondered about it too. Mrs. Rohrshack stated the details would be posted on the website, but I couldn't find it either."

"She mentioned it at the opening ceremony," another volunteer said. "Most organizations detail the judges' names and backgrounds on their website."

The first volunteer scribbled on a piece of paper. "I'll mention it when they ask for suggestions to improve the program."

Immune to the comments, Myaisha stayed focused on Mrs. Newson. The latter hadn't moved.

"Is something wrong, dear?" the second volunteer asked Newson.

As if stung, Newson jerked to attention. "Oh, no. With so much going on, I got distracted."

One of the volunteers made supportive comments.

Myaisha remained steadfast. Because Newson acted disinclined to oblige, she said, "Let me explain why I ask."

She leaned in as if sharing a secret. "I read a post from a member in Charleston who alleged misconduct in the selection process."

Like a row of owls, the volunteers gawked at Myaisha. Each expressed amazement with comments of "No," "What," and "How?"

"I know," Myaisha said, joining in mock disbelief. "Of course, I challenged her assertion by showing her the rules displayed on the website." Her voice lowered once more. "But we couldn't find the judges' names online."

Myaisha's brow rose, and her voice increased an octave. "Then the Charleston member said, 'See, that proves it's rigged.'"

"Must be an oversight," a volunteer said.

Another volunteer nodded.

"First thing in the morning, I told her," Myaisha continued, "I'm going to find Mrs. Newson and get those names and prove you're wrong." Her lips snapped shut with finality.

"Good for you," one of the volunteers said. "We can't have gossips bad-mouthing Fiction Writers of America."

"I agree," another volunteer said.

In concert, all eyes rested on the chairwoman.

In exaggerated slow motion, Newson placed her tote bag on the table. She fished out a binder and flipped through pages of documents. She motioned with her spindly hands for a piece of note paper. For a minute, she scribbled names before handing Myaisha the paper.

"Thank you." Myaisha read the names off audibly. From the corner of her eye, she noticed—as did Mrs. Newson—one of the volunteers taking notes.

"Hmm." She gazed up and left as if considering something. "The website didn't mention how the award selection members are chosen. Could you get us that information?"

A glare shot from Newson's fretful gaze. She slapped the binder on the table. Gritting her teeth, she removed a stapled document.

"Here."

A gigantic smile spread across Myaisha's lips. "I really appreciate it. Everyone has been so helpful."

Before she could depart, one of the volunteers requested a copy. Myaisha accompanied her to the hotel's reception desk. She handed a copy to the volunteer and waved to the others.

Newson did not return the gesture. The woman's downturned mouth testified to her anger. She whipped out a cellphone and stormed away from the registration table.

Wonder who she's calling?

Myaisha got the desired information and managed to create doubt into other attendees. This would provide her with a modicum of protection and amplify scrutiny regarding the Platinum Pen Award.

"Hey."

Lynn's salutation made Myaisha start.

"Morning."

Peering through her strong lenses, Lynn studied the paper in Myaisha's hand.

"I'd like a copy."

They waited silently at the registration desk for the hotelier to copy the document.

"Up early," Lynn said, breaking the silence.

"Are you following me?"

"Of course not," Lynn said, covering her mouth in mocking disbelief. "I would never."

Calmly, Myaisha handed her a copy and thanked the hotelier. To her dismay, Lynn followed as she left the registration desk.

Myaisha halted.

"I'm not interested in your company."

"Did you talk with Mrs. de Jesus?" Lynn asked, dismissive of Myaisha's comment.

"I gave her your card. Take it up with her directly."

"Will do," Lynn said, waving the paper and striding away.

"She's going to be a pain." Myaisha found a bench in the lobby and reviewed the information from Newson.

Whether or not Paige had been murdered because of those concerns, Myaisha believed transparency should be inherent to any organization. FWA had secrets. But had they led to murder?

Chapter 24

From a distance, Myaisha observed Newson cowering behind a potted plant, talking on a cellphone.

In a flash, Newson darted into a waiting elevator. Because of the distance, Myaisha couldn't catch the cab, but she noted the floor where the elevator stopped. She recorded the information for later.

In the lobby, Myaisha phoned Tina.

"I got the judges' names."

"How?"

She explained the confrontation with Newson.

"They're going to be suspicious."

"Deniece and I confronted Rohrshack yesterday. And I questioned Vinson in the afternoon. They know." She purposely omitted mentioning Lynn.

Tina asked, "Do you believe they killed Paige to keep the process secret?"

"Can't be sure."

Myaisha considered what they had uncovered. Paige died suddenly. Authorities found arsenic in her system. And a valuable book had been stolen hours after Paige's death.

But if Paige's symptoms originated in Charleston, would FWA be involved?

Alice mentioned a birthday party. Who attended? Perhaps one of the FWA administrators attended, or they could have mailed Paige a gift. Poison allowed for assassination from a distance. A gift of arsenic? How did Paige ingest the poison?

Myaisha needed to research the chemical properties of arsenic.

"Hello? You there?" Tina asked, raising her voice.

"Sorry. I was wondering about Paige's stolen book."

"I've been thinking. Actually, worrying."

Myaisha realized that if Paige died from arsenic poisoning due to handling a toxic book, no murder had been committed. No murder, no true crime story for Tina. She knew how desperate her friend had become to fulfill her obligation for a second book.

"Worried about the contract?"

"It sounds horrible, but I need a story."

"Tina, we will follow the evidence wherever it leads. Don't pin your future on Paige's death, or on a career as a true crime author."

"I know, but..." A deep inhale preceded Tina saying, "I know."

The call ended.

From the corner of her eye, Myaisha spotted Hunter Vinson entering a conference room. She dropped the cellphone into her tote bag and sprinted across the lobby.

Inside the Marian Wright Edelman Conference Room, Vinson arranged chairs behind a rectangular table at the head of the room.

"Good morning," Myaisha said.

Vinson looked up with a glowing smile, which immediately soured.

"I don't have time to talk." He bustled around the room, straightening chairs and arranging microphones.

"Wednesday night, in the bar, you sounded concerned about Fiction Writers of America's reputation. You mentioned enrollment decreasing."

A full minute passed without him replying.

She leaned against the table. "Paige is dead."

The abrupt statement made Vinson stumble and knock over a chair. He picked it up and gave her a weighty glare.

"Mrs. Goodson was ill. Her death..." He hesitated over the last word, swallowing deeply. "Has nothing to do with me or Fiction Writers of America."

"How do you know it has nothing to do with the organization?"

Vinson frowned. "What do you mean?"

"Are you confident in the integrity of the Platinum Pen Award process?"

Turning his back to her, Vinson sped around the room tidying up the space.

Careful not to betray Detective Salter's intel, Myaisha said, "I could tell from your voice you shared Paige's concerns."

"What if I did?" His voice wavered. "There's nothing I can do about it."

She approached him. "If there's something dishonest in the Platinum Pen Award process, you have to speak up."

He swung around suddenly, catching Myaisha off guard. "And what if I do and no one believes me?"

"There must be proof."

"Proof." His cackle caused goosebumps to erupt along Myaisha's arms. "Like a successful author would confess to collusion in rigging an award contest?"

Was he referring to Tullulah?

"We can find a way."

Vinson's gaze traveled around the room. "Not without destroying my credibility and career."

"It depends upon your level of involvement."

While he stared at the ground, Myaisha studied him. Clean-shaven and impeccably dressed, Hunter Vinson gave off vibes of a CPA financial advisor more than an author.

"What type of books do you write?" she asked.

Energized by her query, Vinson said, "Self-improvement, how-to books."

"Have you been publishing long?"

"Three books over the past five years."

"Quite an accomplishment."

"I think so." A shy smile graced his lips. "At one time, I had a promising career."

Her brows rose in appreciation.

"Even made the top ten once on the biggest book lists in the country."

"Impressive."

"Then my idiot publisher switched editors." His shoulders slumped. "They wanted to go in a new direction." He ran his fingers through his bushy chestnut hair.

"You stopped writing?"

"I stopped publishing, at least books. These days, it's articles, ghost writing. On the fringes of the writing community." He gazed vacantly.

"Your next book could be an exposé on corruption in writing contests."

He chuckled. "You're persuasive."

"Look." She folded her hands. "I'm trying to finish what Paige started. If things are copacetic, great. I'll be Fiction Writers of America's biggest cheerleader."

"And if they aren't?" A sullen tint settled over his face.

"People need to know the truth. Authors rely on organizations to provide transparent, fair contests. Essentially, it's fraud to take authors' money for a contest that is not decided equitably."

"Fraud!" he snarled and advanced toward her.

Cautiously, Myaisha retreated.

"Are you threatening me?"

"No, I'm saying—"

"What? You want me to bear my soul? Sacrifice what infinitesimal career I have left. For what?"

She stumbled over chairs, scrambling for the exit in the rear of the room.

"Paige was a sanctimonious hypocrite."

With her left hand, Myaisha felt around in her purse for a weapon. "This is about the Platinum Pen Award. People will find out what is going on, and those involved will face consequences."

He sneered. "I don't like your tone."

"My point is, when the truth comes out—"

"Truth." He tossed aside a chair between them. "You think I'm going to throw away my career because some," he sized up Myaisha, "wanna-be writer believes she's uncovered improprieties."

"This can stay between us. I simply want to understand how the author of the year is selected."

"Oh, this *will* stay between us." His hands fisted.

Myaisha retreated and bumped into someone. She swung around and gaped.

Chapter 25

Myaisha bumped into Todd. With the touch of his skin, she exhaled. He vaulted in front of her.

Todd charged forward. Vinson jerked to a stop. The men eyeballed each other.

Chest heaving, Vinson said, "I was leaving."

"Thought you were." Todd stepped aside.

Vinson made a wide berth around him, pausing only long enough to send Myaisha a venomous glare.

"Wow." Myaisha adjusted the bag on her shoulder. "Things became ugly real quick."

Todd grinned. "Like a superhero, I arrived right on time."

She gave him a hug. "Thanks."

Together, they exited the room, which began filling with conference attendees awaiting the next program.

"What brings you to Rock Hill?"

He escorted her to a bench in the lobby. "Salter's a friend. I couldn't leave him alone with the Greensboro Women of Color investigative team. He wouldn't survive."

"Ha, ha." Myaisha checked her cellphone. "Not funny."

"No, it wasn't." Todd placed a hand on her shoulder. "That man meant to hurt you."

"He would have quickly discovered his error."

Todd's chin stiffened. "Do you have a death wish?"

"He wouldn't have hurt me, not seriously."

"What do I have to do to convince you to stop investigating homicides?"

Myaisha handed him a piece of chocolate candy. "Technically, it's not a homicide. Not officially, according to the detectives."

Shaking his head, Todd scanned the lobby. "Where's the rest of the brat pack?"

"Upstairs."

They rose and headed for the elevators.

"Where's Ian?" she asked, gazing toward the entrance.

"Home. I didn't want to worry him."

Though she refused to publicly admit it, Myaisha had been delighted to see Todd. Vinson's outburst surprised her and threw her off balance. She'd tussled with a few murderers in the past and did not wish to repeat those experiences.

———————

While they waited for the elevator, Myaisha texted Deniece.

Todd's here. On the way up.

When Deniece failed to reply, she texted Tina.

"So, how's the homicide investigation going?" Todd asked, allowing her to enter the cab first.

"What homicide investigation?"

His forehead creased.

"Unless you've heard differently, the authorities haven't established a murder occurred."

"Disappointing for you all, I'm sure."

Myaisha appreciated the slight upturn at the corner of his lips.

They exited the cabin together.

"I'll explain in the room." She glanced both ways down the hallway, suspicious Lynn might pop out of the walls. "Too many prying eyes."

"And ears." Todd tapped her earlobe.

She waved the keycard across the reader and led him inside.

Tina sprang up from the desk and embraced him. "Hello, Todd."

"Mrs. de Jesus."

"Where's Ian?"

"Greensboro." Todd winked. "I didn't tell him about this adventure."

Tina gave him a peck on the cheek. "Thanks. He worries."

Todd ambled around the suite. "Well, he is a homicide detective. And his mom has a knack for getting involved with murderers."

With a laugh, Tina settled down at the desk. "True crime writing is not an occupational hazard."

"It can be." Todd shot Myaisha a sharp glance.

"Where's Mary?" she asked, placing her tote bag on a side table.

"At a poetry reading or something," Tina said while typing. "I can't remember."

At the window, Todd said, "Catch me up."

Myaisha rested on the couch and explained meeting Alice, how she obtained the judges' names from Tisha Newson, and what occurred with Hunter Vinson before Todd intervened.

"So arsenic could have come from this stolen book." Todd gazed out of the window.

"Possible. Though I can't imagine the pages contained enough arsenic to cause death."

"It would also depend on how Paige handled the book," Tina interjected.

"I would hope she used gloves," Myaisha said.

Tina flicked a stray gray hair off her face. "Her hands might have been damp, or she might have touched her lips."

"Some people lick their fingers between turning pages," Myaisha added.

"All ways to increase the absorption of arsenic." Todd abandoned the window and joined Myaisha on the couch. "Did you tell Salter?"

"Not yet."

A cloud formed over Todd's darkening brow.

"Before you get upset," Myaisha said. "I was waiting until we gathered more information."

"What additional information?" he asked, reclining against the couch cushions. "If Paige acquired the arsenic from this rare book, there's no murder."

"I understand."

"No murder, no investigation."

"And no book," Tina said in a small voice.

Todd took a deep breath and eyed Myaisha.

"We aren't trying to create a murder where one doesn't exist. I intended to call Detective Salter—"

"Now." Todd's heavy brow arched.

"Fine."

Myaisha pulled out her cellphone. She noticed a text from AJ.

Everything okay? Boomer?

Yes. Love U.

Me 2. Call soon.

At least in Greensboro, she could return home and cuddle with AJ—or Boomer. Unfortunately, she didn't expect a positive response from the homicide detective. He would not be pleased about her snooping and interrogating potential suspects.

This would be easier with Deniece.

After a deep breath, she dialed.

"Hello. Rock Hill Homicide Division? May I speak with Detective Salter?"

Chapter 26

Myaisha roamed around the suite while Todd spoke with Detective Salter on her cellphone. He placed it on speaker.

"No one reported a stolen book," Detective Salter said.

"Do you know how to contact this Alice person?" Todd asked Myaisha.

She turned to Tina. "Do you have her number?"

The latter nodded.

"I'll reach out to her. If this book contains arsenic, this case is closed," Detective Salter said.

Todd grinned. "It'll make for a quieter weekend."

"Thanks for the information, Doc," Detective Salter said. "I wonder why the sister didn't report the theft."

"Did you check with the hotel?" Todd asked. "She might have notified them first."

"Good point. Will work on it." Detective Salter addressed Myaisha, "Pass on anything you learn. Keep your ears open, but don't approach anyone else. We might be able to close this case without making our suspicions public."

"Fat chance," Todd said, handing Myaisha the cellphone.

"Excuse me?" the detective asked.

"Ignore Todd's poor attempt at humor." Myaisha promised to let the detective know if they learned anything else and hung up.

She stared vacantly at the wall. "Why didn't Alice inform the police of the theft?"

Tina swiveled her chair around. "The *Antiquarium Botanique* is rare and expensive."

"Paige is—was," Myaisha corrected, "rich. Perhaps Alice neglected to call the police because she doesn't care about the money."

"But the book was for a client, correct?" Todd asked.

"True." Myaisha's forehead creased in thought.

"Maybe the buyer hadn't paid yet," Tina suggested.

Myaisha removed her fedora, placing it delicately on the coffee table. "Alice would have to explain to the buyer why the book couldn't be delivered."

Silence filled the room as they each pursued their separate thoughts.

Todd asked, "Wouldn't Alice want help retrieving such an expensive book?"

"She's in mourning. Hadn't considered it yet," Tina suggested.

"Stolen property can't be reported to the police without admitting culpability." Myaisha watched Todd.

Tina shook her head. "Alice didn't strike me as a thief."

"What about Paige?" Myaisha observed Tina's reaction.

"Why would a successful businesswoman risk jail time to sell books?"

"Paige owned a bookstore," Myaisha said. "She might have been trading in black market books to supplement her income. Bookstores have struggled in this economy."

"If people can't afford rent," Todd said, "they cut back on non-essentials."

Fingering her fedora, Myaisha agreed. "Alice said Paige was successful, but we don't know if those enterprises were legitimate."

Tina paled. "I don't like where this is headed."

Todd extended his arms along the couch. "Murder usually involves associated illegal activities."

Myaisha reviewed her list. "We have questions only one person can answer."

"I know where April is staying." Tina rose and handed Myaisha a torn piece of paper. "She wanted to be contacted if we learned anything."

"About the book or her sister?" Todd asked.

"I presumed about her sister's death." Tina's chin quivered.

"We didn't tell Alice we suspected Paige had been murdered," Myaisha said.

Todd grinned with a rise in his right eyebrow. "Want to go for a ride?"

Chapter 27

Five miles off the interstate, Todd entered an apartment enclave. Magnolia trees lined the entrance. Myaisha watched birds playing tag around waxy verdant leaves. She longed for her Greensboro wide porch with its blue beadboard ceiling, sipping tea beside AJ while Boomer and Zoey chased each other in the backyard.

Her chest sighed. She wanted AJ and needed Deniece.

How can I protect my best friend and explain to AJ I need more intimacy?

"Which way?" Todd asked as they passed a row of mailboxes.

Myaisha provided directions. "This is it," she said, unbuckling the seatbelt.

Todd grabbed her arm. "Let me lead. This isn't official, but if a crime has been committed, I don't want to mess up a potential police investigation."

"Always a cop."

"It would be nice if you would always be a doctor," he quipped, "and not play amateur investigator."

Myaisha winced.

At the green door, Todd knocked and stepped to the side, positioning Myaisha slightly behind him.

He worries about me.

The door opened. In plaid pajama bottoms, an unshaven man asked, "Yeah?"

Over Todd's shoulder, she said, "I'm Myaisha, a friend of Alice. Actually, a friend of her sister, Paige."

"I'm Tad."

"Please accept our condolences."

Todd asked, "May we come in?"

"Oh, sure." Tad opened the door wider, directing them forward. "Alice mentioned you were looking into her sister's death." With a questioning brow, the man regarded Todd.

"I'm transportation," Todd said, crossing the threshold.

Tad preceded them into a great room combining the living area and kitchen. He yelled, "Alice! Someone to see you. It's about Paige."

Sounds from an unseen room preceded Alice bustling into the living room. "Good morning."

They shook hands.

Myaisha introduced Todd. "This is a friend from Greensboro."

"Nice to meet you." Alice signaled for them to be seated. "Would you like something to drink? Water—"

"I'll make coffee," Tad said, retiring to the kitchen.

Myaisha scooted to the edge of the chair. "Alice, I don't want to upset you."

Alice's enormous blue eyes fastened on Myaisha. "What did you find out?"

Unable to find a delicate way to broach the topic, she asked, "Did you notify the police about the stolen book?"

Strain wrinkled Alice's forehead. "No. I've been too disturbed by Paige's death."

"Have you considered it may be the cause of her death?"

"Can't be. Paige..." Tremulous, Alice started to rise. Her eyelids fluttered.

Afraid Alice might faint, Myaisha rose.

"I'll get a glass of water." Todd rushed into the kitchen.

Myaisha guided Alice to a couch. She raised Alice's feet onto a pillow.

Cradling her hand, Myaisha said, "There's a chance Paige's death is related to the book."

"Arsenic?"

She nodded.

Alice bolted upright. "Paige always wore gloves when handling the books."

"Always," Tad said, returning with coffee.

Arabica wafted around the room as Tad handed around mugs.

Myaisha set hers aside. She detested coffee.

After two sips, Alice said, "Paige was extremely careful handling the books. With what they cost, she said we had to be cautious. Oils from our hands could damage the pages."

"You helped Paige sell books?" Todd asked, taking a seat across from Myaisha.

Tad and Alice exchanged a surreptitious glance. The latter set the coffee mug down with a bang.

"You should go." Alice rushed toward the front door.

Todd scrutinized Tad, who stared sheepishly at his feet.

"There's a valuable book stolen the same day a vibrant, active woman suddenly dies." Todd's gaze fastened on Tad.

Myaisha hovered between the living room and front door, unsure of what to do and not wanting to interfere with Todd's momentum. "We're here as friends, seeking justice for Paige."

Alice held the front door open. "You didn't even know her."

Keeping his eyes on the boyfriend, Todd rose. "Once we leave, the police will interrogate you both about the suspicious circumstances surrounding the theft from your sister's hotel room."

Without raising his head, Tad said, "I didn't do anything wrong."

Myaisha approached Alice. "No one has to get into trouble. We simply need to understand Paige's business."

As if a switch had flipped, Tad animated. He addressed Myaisha. "Can you get the book back?"

Before she could answer, Todd asked Tad, "Did you tell the buyer it had been stolen?"

"Not yet."

"Shut up!" Alice abandoned the door and raced over to Tad.

"I'm not getting into trouble to protect your precious sister's reputation."

The nymph morphed into a harpy. Alice's nostrils flared. "Be quiet. I can handle this."

"Since when?" He chuckled. "You did nothing. Paige and I managed the transactions. All you did was spend the profits."

Smack.

Tad's cheek glowed with April's bright red handprint. His chest heaved. "You'll regret that, Princess."

Before he stormed into the bedroom, Tad handed Todd a card. "Call me if you find the book. There'll be a nice reward for your efforts."

Seconds passed as Myaisha and Todd waited. A crimson flush covered Alice's neck.

"My sister was not a thief," Alice said in answer to their scrutiny.

"Where did the books come from?" Todd asked.

"I..." Alice swallowed half of the glass of water. "Paige and Tad oversaw the rare book sales. My sister thought it would be prudent for me to remain ignorant about certain aspects of the business."

Myaisha guided Alice to a chair. "She wanted to protect you."

"Always." Tears brimmed along Alice's eyelids. "Tad worked in Paige's bookstore before it closed."

"He's not your boyfriend," she said.

Alice shook her head.

"Once she sold the bookstore, your sister continued the business offline," Todd concluded.

"Pretty much." Alice drank water, cupping the glass in her trembling hands.

"Did the buyer threaten you?"

"Tad received a threatening email." Alice set down the glass. "The buyer suspected we had double-crossed them. Accepting their finder's fee but selling the book to another collector for a larger commission."

"Did you return the finder's fee?" Todd asked.

"We tried!" Alice shrieked. "They're demanding the book or else."

"Had Paige ever been threatened before?" Myaisha asked.

"My sister dealt fairly with everyone." Because she shook her head so rapidly, tears flew around Alice's shoulders. "I know it sounds hypocritical, but Paige believed in honesty. These books weren't stolen. The sellers wanted to remain anonymous—"

"To cheat on their income tax or hide assets," Todd interjected.

"It didn't hurt anyone."

Simply cheated the government.

"Are these people—or this person—coming after Tad?" Todd asked.

Alice nodded. "The buyer is wealthy and connected."

He began to remove a cellphone from his coat pocket.

Alice grabbed his hand. "Don't."

Todd shook himself free.

"Please. It will cause so many problems."

"For you?" Todd glared at her.

Tad exited the bedroom dressed in jeans and a T-shirt. "I'm going to the police."

"Wait." Alice dashed between him and the door.

"It's not your head the buyer will come after, darling." He shoved her aside.

"Give me until the weekend," Alice pleaded.

Myaisha asked, "Why are you so worried about Paige's reputation?"

"She's not." Tad opened the front door. "If the police investigate, they might notify the IRS, and Paige's estate will have to pay back taxes on our transaction fees."

Alice shouted, "You'll have to pay back taxes, too!"

"I'd rather face the IRS than a hedge fund manager with a grievance."

Outside, Todd caught up with Tad in the parking lot. Myaisha remained on the front porch.

Swaying slightly, Alice leaned against the door frame beside Myaisha. "To you, I look like a coward."

"You're human." Myaisha patted her arm. "We're going to look into your sister's death."

"And the book?"

"If we find it, we'll call."

Even as the words left her mouth, Myaisha knew the odds of finding the missing book were slim to none. Whoever took the book sold it or hid it, likely not in the hotel. And yet, Myaisha remained uncertain of the book's role in Paige's death.

Things looked so simple at first.

With each passing hour, the mystery surrounding Paige's death grew legs like a deadly black widow.

Chapter 28

Parked in front of the hotel, Todd set the emergency brake and glanced at Myaisha. "You sure know how to show a guy a good time."

She grinned. "This time *you* got the ball rolling."

"True." His long fingers tapped the steering wheel, reminding Myaisha of the Christmas concert where Todd elegantly delivered a solo piano performance. "What next?"

"Check in with the team."

"Keep me informed."

Myaisha started to exit the car. "How about you?"

"I'm heading over to speak with Salter."

"Make sure to tell him you got this information from Tad, not me."

"Will do." Todd saluted. "Be safe."

"Count on it."

Todd made a dour face and drove off.

The blast of air conditioning inside the hotel made Myaisha shiver.

Or could it be a premonition?

Minutes passed. She hovered beside the entrance, surveying the lobby. Neither a person nor a thought provided inspiration.

She observed the hotel registration desk. Travelers scurried around, departing for home or distant lands. Conference attendees chatted, gliding effortlessly between events.

Many possibilities surrounded Paige's death. And the authorities had yet to confirm a homicide. Tina needed it to be a murder, but...

Had Paige been murdered, or had she succumbed to the arsenic from the *Antiquarium Botanique*? Tad *and* Alice insisted Paige wore gloves while handling the toxic tome. If they were to be believed, Paige had been murdered with arsenic. Was the murderer's choice of poison coincidental?

Without knowing the delivery mechanism for the poison, the answer remained elusive.

Tired, Myaisha headed up to the hotel room.

"Hey guys." She tossed her purse on the table next to the FWA tote bag. "Anything new?"

Tina stopped typing and handed Myaisha a writing pad. Her raised brows questioned its purpose.

"Research on the judges," Tina said.

"Nice." Myaisha settled on the couch and read. "Is a judge on the award committee from the Palmetto Writers group?"

"Yep." Tina closed the browser.

"I don't want to hear this." Mary gathered her sweater and tote bag. "Greg will be furious if I get involved in another homicide."

"And you do everything he tells you to do?" Tina smirked.

"We're here to participate in a writing conference. Period." Mary headed for the door. "Besides, there's an author round table in ten minutes."

"Wait." Tina shoved her laptop into a backpack. "I'm coming."

"Doesn't Fiction Writers of America have rules about relationships between judges and contest participants?" Myaisha asked while reading.

"Supposedly," Tina said. "Perhaps they recused themselves from reading books submitted from authors in their writing group."

"One of the judges was a developmental editor on two Tullulah Bishop books."

"According to the information I found, at least two judges have, or had, a direct relationship with Tullulah Bishop."

Myaisha's nose wrinkled. "Smells rotten."

"Looks hinky," Tina said. "And one of the judges is part of the Palmetto Writers critique group."

"Bye." Mary opened the door.

"Hold up," Tina said.

"Hurry."

"I tripped someone to get you an interview with an editor. The least you can do is wait a minute."

"It's been several minutes, and I didn't tell you to trip her," Mary said, defiantly raising her head.

"You didn't bend down to help her up."

"We're gonna be late."

Tina asked, "Myaisha, aren't you going to attend any programs?"

"Hmm?"

"Myaisha?"

"She's stuck on Paige's murder." Mary grabbed Tina's hand. "Let's go."

The door closed.

How could FWA allow a member of Palmetto Writers to judge an author from their writing group? Administration must be complicit in this arrangement.

"How much of this had Paige uncovered?" Myaisha asked. Not getting a response, she looked up. "Guys?"

She searched each bedroom. "Where did they go?" Next, she texted Deniece.

Where are you?

Seconds later, she received a response with a smiley face.

None of your business.

She phoned Deniece, who answered on the first ring. "Where's my partner?"

"Miss me?"

"I thought you were helping me," Myaisha said, collapsing on the couch.

"When I woke up, you were gone and left no messages."

"Todd and I went to talk with April."

"Oh, baby." Deniece made a loud puckering sound and sang, "Todd and Myaisha sitting in a tree."

"Seriously. Stop." She sat up. "I want to talk over the case."

"And I want to attend a workshop on marketing."

"What happened to 'I'm happily self-published.'"

"People regard self-publishing with the same disdain they have for homeschooling. Like we're antisocial freaks," Deniece retorted. "I want to grow, increase my exposure, and profits."

"Are you going to help me or not?"

"Call your boyfriend."

"AJ—"

"Todd. Your side piece."

"He's not..." Hearing the dial tone, Myaisha hung up.

Undecided about what infuriated her more, Deniece's abandonment or taunting about Todd, Myaisha reclined on the couch, staring up at the ceiling. In time, her eyelids lagged.

Visions of books danced in her head. She watched a contest on television where prizes were awarded. The audience applauded for each contestant. One person won a pencil, another a tote bag. In her dream, Myaisha received a gift box with an elaborate bow. She opened it, and green slime poured over her hands.

The box fell from her trembling hands. Pustules erupted along her fingers and crept up her arms. Upset, Myaisha looked for somewhere to cleanse her hands. In the distance, she discerned a whistle. It sounded more like a bell ringing.

With a start, Myaisha awoke. A number flashed across her cellphone screen.

"Hi Todd," she said, sitting up.

"Things okay?" he asked. "I've called three times."

"Sorry. I fell asleep."

"I was about to head over there and make sure nothing happened to my favorite amateur sleuth."

He really is a considerate friend. Or did he want to be more than friends?

"Myaisha?"

"Give me a moment. I'm still waking up."

"We're on speaker phone. Salter's here."

She rubbed sleep from her eyes. "Hello, Detective. Did Todd explain what we learned from Tad?"

"The boyfriend?"

"I don't believe he's her boyfriend," Myaisha corrected.

"He made an official report of a stolen book, explaining about arsenic in the cover. Apparently, there's a huge underground market for rare poisonous books."

"People are bizarre," Todd said.

"Whatever keeps them busy and out of my hair," Detective Salter continued. "Anyway, I shared the information with the chief. Goodson's death will officially be classified as accidental."

"Why?"

Todd said, "Myaisha, the book is covered in arsenic. The woman had arsenic in her system. In other words, an accident."

"Enough to cause a precipitous death at a writers conference?"

"Yes," both Todd and Detective Salter said in unison.

"Both Alice and Tad insist Paige wore gloves when handling the books."

"Mistakes happen."

Myaisha reevaluated what she knew about arsenic. "It's unlikely Paige would consume enough arsenic to explain her violent death if she religiously used gloves like her sister explained. A slow, drawn-out death, perhaps. But this illness occurred within days."

"Exceptions occur," Detective Salter said. "Not every death follows the rules."

"Shouldn't you wait until the official toxicology report returns?" Myaisha asked. "The level of toxicity might settle whether Paige's death was accidental or intentional."

In an aside, Todd said, "See what I have to put up with."

"I do," Detective Salter said.

Myaisha imagined the two men sharing stories about their interactions with her and Deniece. "Excuse me for interrupting the bromance, but a woman is dead. And we need answers."

"*We* have answered the question surrounding Mrs. Goodson's death," Detective Salter asserted. "Enjoy the writers' conference and stand down. Amateur hour is over."

An itch grew in Myaisha's brain to express her opinion of the detective's conclusion. In deference to Todd, she refrained.

"Understood." She realized no further cooperation would come from Rock Hill Homicide.

"And you will drop the investigation," the detective stated.

"Goodbye, Detective. I appreciate your assistance."

Before Myaisha ended the call, she heard Todd say, "Dude, it's not over."

Chapter 29

Myaisha tucked the cellphone in her pocket and gazed out the window at Rock Hill. The balmy summer day almost made her want to take a walk. Almost.

Without Boomer or AJ, she had no desire to exercise. But she did need to refresh her mind. No Deniece or detectives.

How am I going to solve this alone?

Tina would help, but she had ulterior motives. Could Myaisha rely on her to be objective?

Lynn? The true crime author had a rabid zeal which discouraged cooperation.

AJ? He hated mysteries and would pester her about investigating another homicide.

She yawned and extended her legs along the couch. "Start at the beginning. Paige suspected the Platinum Pen Award process had been rigged. Next, she arranged to meet with the organization's president. Then she dies on a bathroom floor ostensibly from arsenic poisoning."

Myaisha scribbled notes on a writing pad. "To-do list. Why didn't the Fiction Writers of America president attend the conference?"

Needing stimulation, she circled the sitting area, voicing her ideas. "Wait. Paige mentioned on her blog about the upcoming meeting. Why didn't the president contact Paige and cancel?"

Resting on the edge of the couch, Myaisha braided her thick black tendrils. "Maybe she had, and Paige didn't get the message. But on the rooftop deck, Paige sounded surprised by the president's decision not to attend the conference."

Myaisha wandered into the bedroom, looking for something to tie off the braids. "Or the president told someone to notify Paige about the last-minute cancellation, and that person withheld the message."

In the living room, Myaisha continued listing possibilities and questions.

"Paige traded in rare valuable books. She brought the *Antiquarium Botanique* to the conference and intended to sell it. The buyer could be a member of Fiction Writers of America or a person attending the conference."

She sent a quick text to AJ and boiled water for tea.

"Who would know Paige had a rare book?"

Top of the list, Myaisha wrote the names *Alice* and *Tad*.

"Paige's roommate might have known." Myaisha reviewed her notes. "What's the woman's name?"

The suite door opened, and Deniece entered.

"Hey, girl."

"Hey?" Myaisha stood. "Where have you been?"

"Excuse me, mom," Deniece said, placing a hand on her hip, "but I've been learning how to network and grow my online business."

Myaisha tossed her pencil onto the table. "I didn't mean it like that."

"Get off the couch and get downstairs." Deniece hurried into the bedroom. "There's an author meet and greet at five."

"What about Paige?"

Deniece unbuttoned her blouse and draped it over the bed. She shed her clothing and headed for the shower. "Leave it to the police."

"They believe poison from the book caused Paige's death."

Water blasted from the shower head. Steam gradually filled the bathroom.

"Sounds about right."

"Don't you care?" Myaisha asked, standing beside the bathroom door.

"Not my job." Deniece tapped Myaisha's nose. "Not yours either." She shut the door in her friend's face.

"Why are you taking a shower for a meet and greet?"

"I want to appear at my best."

"Since when did you care what people thought?" Myaisha meandered into the shared living area and resumed her list of information gathered and questions to be answered.

Time passed, and eventually, Deniece exited the bedroom and executed a twirl, sending a spicy perfume fragrance around the room. "How do I look?" The vivid red dress with an empire waist accentuated the nurse's curvy figure.

With a brief glance, Myaisha said, "Too dressy for a group of strangers."

Deniece cocked her head to the side. "We can't all be slouches."

Myaisha inspected her attire. "This is comfy casual."

"Lies you tell yourself."

She scowled at Deniece.

"Should I wear makeup? Naw, why gild the lily." Deniece slipped a shawl over her bare shoulders. "I'm off. Call your boyfriend if you need a sidekick."

"Wait." Myaisha dashed between Deniece and the door. "We need to talk about last night."

"No, we don't." Deniece started to leave.

"At the bar—"

Deniece swiveled around. "Mind your business."

"You are my business."

They glared at each other. A ringing phone broke the détente. Both women checked their phones.

Myaisha said, "It's AJ."

"Tell the firefighter about your feelings for Todd."

The door to the suite shut behind Deniece before Myaisha could respond.

After speaking with AJ, Myaisha settled on the couch and considered options.

Chase after my best friend before she destroys a happy marriage, or investigate a suspicious death the police are classifying as an accident.

"I need a drink."

The water for her tea had evaporated.

Myaisha reached into the tote bag. "Where's my water bottle?"

She dumped out the bag's contents. Other than the welcome packet, she didn't recognize any of the items: makeup, lotion, and a medication bottle. Like the sun rising over a mountain, a realization dawned on her.

"This isn't my tote bag. It belonged to Paige."

Chapter 30

Cross-legged sitting on the floor, Myaisha watched Detective Salter, Detective Cambell, and Todd inspect Paige's tote bag. They displayed each item on the coffee table.

"And you've been carrying this around since Thursday?" Detective Cambell asked.

"I had no idea." Myaisha returned the detective's harsh glare. "Why would I withhold evidence?"

"Um, let me see." Detective Cambell pretended to be considering ideas. "To help your friend with her true crime book. To be a pain in the neck and interfere with our investigation."

"Didn't I call you as soon as I figured out it wasn't mine?"

"For a clever sleuth, it seems like a stupid oversight not to notice the tote bag belonged to the deceased." Detective Cambell turned his back to her.

"All attendees received the same bag. The one thing I used it for was carrying the welcome packet and my thermos."

He scoffed. "Until this evening."

"I wanted some water. The first day of the conference, I stuck my water bottle in the tote bag."

Detective Salter said, "So, when Mrs. Goodson collapsed..."

"Paige looked like she was going to pass out." Myaisha closed her eyes, bringing the events of the bathroom to the forefront of her consciousness. "I helped her to the floor, checked vitals, ran to the door, and yelled into the lobby for someone to call 911."

"When did you pick up the tote bag?" Todd asked.

Needing a friendly face, Myaisha looked at him. "EMTs arrived. People poured into the bathroom. In the commotion, I must have picked up the wrong one."

Todd addressed Detective Salter. "Easy to prove. Myaisha's tote bag should be with Goodson's effects."

"The sister picked them up," Detective Cambell said, shooting Myaisha another glare.

Detective Salter said, "No, she didn't."

Everyone gawked at him.

"The sister came by and viewed the items but didn't take anything. Forensics searched Goodson's hotel room for items related to a possible poisoning. Clothing, shoes, and books all remained at the hotel," he said.

Barely a beat passed before Detective Cambell phoned the police department.

"We'll check the station," Detective Salter said. "If the tote bag contains an aluminum water bottle, your story tracks."

"What about this stuff?" Myaisha asked, surveying the items on the coffee table.

Using a clear plastic bag, Detective Salter gathered the items. "Forensics will check them for arsenic."

After ending his call, Detective Cambell gave a slight lift of his chin to his partner.

"They found your water bottle in the tote bag downtown," Todd told Myaisha.

She exhaled. "Good."

Detective Cambell said, "I can't believe all this time you were carrying around evidence." He departed, shaking his head.

"I apologize." Myaisha cradled her head in her hands.

Todd rested a hand on her shoulder. "No harm done. It delayed things a day or two. Forensics likely wouldn't have conducted their analysis until Monday."

She looked up and gave him a tepid grin.

Detective Salter asked, "Anything else you're holding back, deliberately or accidentally?"

"Detective, I've shared everything I know and have."

"Okay." He shook her hand. "We'll take it from here." Detective Salter gave Todd a nod and left.

Myaisha slumped onto the couch. Todd joined her a moment later. Neither looked at each other nor spoke for several minutes.

"Crazy day," Todd said, stretching his arms along the couch.

"This entire trip has been insane."

He chuckled. "And I thought it was something about Greensboro that led you to crime. Turns out you sniff out homicides wherever you go."

She relaxed against the couch cushions. "All I wanted this weekend was to hone my craft and learn more about Fiction Writers of America for our writing group."

Todd patted her knee. "Don't worry. It's not your fault murders attract you like a magnet."

The twinkle in his eye warmed her heart. He understood the allure of mysteries. The desire to find a conclusion. They shared a passion for puzzles and chocolate. A part of her psyche AJ couldn't appreciate. She and Todd discussed true crime stories and swapped thriller novels.

It wasn't cheating to share interests with a man other than AJ. Was it?

Myaisha escorted Todd to the door. He gave her a peck on the cheek.

"Stay safe." He left.

Her fingers caressed the area he'd kissed. Did Todd care for her beyond friendship?

She thought they had settled this. Of course, neither specifically stated how they felt.

I thought Todd understood my affection for him was platonic.

For seconds, Myaisha hovered beside the door, conflicted about following Todd and clarifying their relationship. She didn't want to upset him, nor jeopardize a solid friendship. But she needed to be clear.

Why do problems multiply like rabbits?

From inside the hotel room, a phone rang. Myaisha answered on the second ring.

"Ready for dinner?" Tina asked.

"I want to go to the barbecue place," Mary said.

Tina said, "If we hurry, we can get back before the main ceremony tonight."

"Tonight?" Myaisha asked.

"The Platinum Pen Award ceremony is tonight at eight."

"It completely slipped my mind."

"Grab Deniece and let's go," Mary said.

Myaisha had forgotten about her friend. "I'll look for D. Y'all grab dinner. Get us a to-go tray."

Once the call ended, Myaisha stuffed her cellphone and room key card in her pants pocket.

"I'm not letting my best friend throw away her marriage."

The occupied elevators were taking too long. Impatient, Myaisha scrambled into the stairwell. The musty smell made her anxious to exit.

Garbled voices ricocheted off cement walls. The heated exchange made Myaisha slow down, but she couldn't understand their words. A door to another floor opened, and conversations ceased.

Interested, Myaisha hesitated, hoping the conversation would resume. A minute passed. Nothing.

Forget it.

Less than a minute later, she burst onto the lobby floor.

Where's Deniece?

Once she'd scanned each conference room, Myaisha headed for the bar, suspicious her best friend had lied about the author meet-up.

Deniece wouldn't dress up for a group of authors, but she might for her bearded admirer.

Unlike Friday night, the bar sat empty except for a handful of people. The bartender saluted, beckoning Myaisha with a wave of his hand. She approached.

He leaned across the bar. "What can I get you?"

"I'm looking for a friend." She described Deniece, including the red dress.

"Nope. No one like that in here today."

Myaisha rested on a stool, considering where to check next.

The bartender placed his hand over hers. "How about a drink, on the house?"

"No thanks." She bustled out of the bar.

Why am I attracting every man but the one I want?

"One more place to check."

Myaisha waited at the elevators for a ride up to the eighth floor. On the short trip, she considered what to say.

How do I convince Deniece not to ruin her life over a weekend tryst?

"Maybe I should try calling again?"

Myaisha stepped out of the elevator and off to the side. She let the cellphone ring until it went to voicemail.

"Of course, she's not answering. Too busy canoodling."

Three treks up and down the carpeted hallway, and she had yet to come up with a plan.

"This is ridiculous. I'm going to the room."

Rounding the corner and heading for room 812, Myaisha bumped into a utility cart. It tilted, spilling debris across the hallway.

"I'm so sorry," the maid said.

"It was my fault."

She helped pick up dropped towels and rolls of toilet paper, assisting the maid in clearing the passageway. At the same time, Myaisha swiped a card key from the cart. With sincere apologies, she departed.

Once the maid entered a room farther down the hall, Myaisha glanced at the card key in her hand. Like a thief, she prowled the hallway a fifth and sixth time.

"If you're gonna do this, do it."

With a surge of courage, or stupidity, Myaisha swiped the key card against the reader and charged into room 812.

Lit but empty, the living area showed no signs of occupancy. She realized Deniece and the bearded man were either not there or were in the bedroom. A giggle from the bedroom confirmed their location.

Inching down the entryway, Myaisha considered phoning Deniece as the bedroom door burst open.

"Just a moment. Let me get some champagne." Deniece scampered from the bedroom and smacked right into Myaisha.

"What the hell are you doing?" Deniece asked, wearing pink sheer lingerie.

Myaisha snatched her friend's arm and dragged her toward the front door.

"Stopping you from making a horrible mistake," Myaisha whispered.

"How did you find out about this room?" Deniece asked, poking her in the chest.

"Doesn't matter. We're leaving."

Deniece swatted Myaisha's arm away. "You've been following me."

"It was an accident." Myaisha stuttered. "I was in the bar—"

"Since when do you go to bars?" Deniece eyed Myaisha.

"Listen." Myaisha continued to push her toward the door. "We can fight later."

Planting her feet, Deniece refused to budge. "You sanctimonious—"

"What's going on?" a male voice asked.

Goosebumps sprouted along Myaisha's arms. The last thing she wanted was to confront her married best friend's lover. She begged Deniece.

"Please. Let's go."

"You're going to regret this," Deniece said, prying Myaisha's hands from her forearm.

"No, you are." Myaisha's neck became taut as she implored. "A wonderful man who adores the ground you walk on is waiting in North Carolina, and you throw it away for what?"

"Myaisha. What are you doing here?"

Recognizing the voice, Myaisha swung around.

"Barry?" Puzzlement etched across her forehead. Deniece's husband, who supposedly had remained behind in Greensboro, wore an artificial beard, mustache, and a wig of dreadlocks.

"I..." Her face crumbled. "Umm..."

Deniece shouted. "Get out!"

Myaisha fled.

Chapter 31

Boxes and bags of food coated every surface of the hotel suite's living room. A heavy scent of barbecue hung in the air. Myaisha licked spicy tomatoey sauce off her fingers.

"Thanks, guys." She wiped her hands on a towelette. "I needed this."

Tina leaped from the chair. "We should get dressed. The ceremony starts in an hour."

"Are seats reserved?" Mary asked.

"Yes, but I want to be present for the entire event." Tina dashed into their separate bedroom.

"It's not like they have previews," Mary said, following after her. "This isn't a movie theater."

Alone in the living room, Myaisha cleared away takeout containers. Fat and grease comforted her wounded spirit.

How could I have suspected Deniece of cheating on Barry? She'll never forgive me for this. And Barry...

"He probably thinks I'm an idiot—or a voyeur."

Myaisha sauntered into her bedroom and collapsed on the bed.

What a weekend.

"I investigated a homicide, which is likely an accident, alienated myself from the Fiction Writers of America organization's administration, and I snooped on my best friend. Perfect."

She considered calling AJ, but his shift didn't end until tomorrow morning.

"He wouldn't mind, though."

"Hurry," Tina called from the other bedroom.

"I don't want to go," she moaned.

Mary bolted through the doorway. "Why not? Is this because of Paige?"

How can I explain feeling like dirt for accusing Deniece of philandering?

"I ate a lot. My stomach hurts."

Tina chuckled. "Liar. I've seen you eat twice as much."

"Get dressed," Mary said, tossing a dress on the bed beside Myaisha's head. "We'll be late."

"Y'all go ahead." Myaisha dragged herself off the bed. "I'll come down later."

Tina and Mary shouted from the living room.

"You better."

"Or we'll come and get you."

Once they left, Myaisha showered and dressed. The one mandate she had for this trip was to determine if the Greensboro Women of

Color Writing Group should join FWA. At least she could successfully accomplish one thing this weekend.

Elegantly dressed attendees flowed into the Mary McLeod Bethune Ballroom. Women wore floor-length dresses bedazzled with sequins. Men sported suits with cuff links.

Tina checked their tickets. "Our table is number fourteen."

At a slower pace, Myaisha followed.

Multicolored decorations animated the room. Silver and gold balloons hovered above their heads. Streamers and posters announced FWA and their Platinum Pen Award ceremony in bold cursive lettering.

"They put a lot of effort into this event," Myaisha said to no one in particular.

"Of course they did," a woman wearing a silver ballroom dress answered. "Platinum Pen is the most respected author prize in the country."

Raised brows gave a silent reply as Myaisha continued toward table fourteen. In the crowd, Myaisha noticed Joyce. "Hi."

Joyce twitched and almost dropped her tote bag.

Myaisha instinctively reached forward. "I didn't mean to startle you." She scanned the floor. "Did you lose anything?"

"I don't think so."

Her gaze fixed on Joyce's tote bag, remembering how she'd mistakenly carried Paige's around for the past two days.

"Are you enjoying the festivities?"

"Definitely," Joyce said, pulling the bag closer to her side.

"Planning a trip to Australia?" Myaisha pointed at a brochure peeking out of the tote bag.

"Another writing conference."

"Wow," she said. "On the other side of the world."

"Paige and I visited New Zealand before." Joyce's countenance clouded, and her head slumped slightly.

Myaisha laid a hand on her shoulder. "My condolences. I understand you two were close."

As if electrified by the touch, Joyce's shoulder shot up. "Yes. Well, I must be going." She bolted away before Myaisha could respond.

Surprised, Myaisha watched Joyce.

What did I say? Did I insult her?

People navigated around Myaisha as she stood in the middle of the walkway.

"Where shall we sit?" Mary asked, circling around their assigned table.

Myaisha chose a chair from where she could view the entrance. Tina and Mary sat on opposite sides of her.

Tonight, I've insulted Deniece and Joyce. Forget winning Ms. Congeniality.

Crestfallen, Myaisha perused the evening's program listed on the invitation.

A physician should possess better people skills.

"This is exciting," Mary said, sipping water.

"Is this award as nationally recognized as this ceremony would suggest?" she asked.

"No." Tina placed her handbag on the table. "But don't tell them."

Myaisha studied the rapturous gazes of attendees. "Their devotion appears extreme."

In time, their table filled with other participants. Myaisha scanned the room for the Palmetto Writers. It took several minutes, but she located them seated at a table close to the presentation platform. She pointed them out.

"I'm not surprised they're seated up front," Tina said. "Tullulah has won more often than any other author."

"Humph," interjected a gentleman seated at their table. "Her luck ends tonight."

"Oh." Tina sat up straight. "Have you entered?"

He shook his head and tilted toward the heavily made-up woman beside him. "My wife expects to bring the prize home tonight. Right, sweetheart?"

"Don't jinx me." The woman lightly tapped his hand. She leaned forward across the table. "This is my third time entering."

"Three's a charm," her enthusiastic companion added.

"Good luck," Myaisha said. Her gaze returned to the Palmetto Writers.

Would Tullulah win again? Paige would have been incredulous.

Myaisha shook her head free of Paige and murder. For once, she would concentrate on writing, authors, and books. Curiosity had already created a fissure in her relationship with Deniece.

How can I apologize for suspecting her of adultery?

Deniece was right about crime solving becoming an addiction. Besides ruining your own life, it destroyed relationships. There had to be a way to mend their friendship. She'd already lost her husband and oldest friend. To now lose Deniece would be devastating.

"Don't you think?" Mary asked.

Myaisha focused on her friend. "My mind was elsewhere."

"I know where your mind was." Tina glanced over at a table in front of the speaker's platform where the Palmetto Writers congregated.

"Actually, my mind was on Deniece," she said.

Mary frowned. "Where is she? We haven't seen her today."

Myaisha could tell them, but not without revealing how she had walked in on Deniece and Barry engaged in romantic role play.

I guess that's how they keep the spark alive.

Lately, there hadn't been any sparks in her relationship with AJ—not even a fizzle. Between his full-time job and part-time business rehabilitating old homes, they had no opportunity for romance.

Did I want sparks?

Applause erupted, drawing Myaisha's gaze to the platform. Attendees stood as three people strode across the stage, waving their hands and sending out hand-shaped hearts like pageant contestants.

"Good evening." Mrs. Rohrshack carried a microphone and gestured for people to be seated. "Welcome, Fiction Writers of America members."

Several shouts and whoops followed. Over the next few minutes, applause diminished, and people returned to their seats. Hunter Vinson and Tisha Newson stood slightly left of center. Their glowing plastic smiles eclipsed even Mrs. Rohrshack.

Once the praise faded, Mrs. Rohrshack welcomed Vinson and Newson to her side.

"This is the Fiction Writers of America award ceremony gala," Mrs. Rohrshack said. "Each year, our awards committee gathers to review books for the Platinum Pen Award."

Though she paused for effect, the audience didn't react. Mrs. Rohrshack continued. "This year, we received over two hundred submissions."

Amid tepid applause, Myaisha declined a plate from a server.

Likewise, Mary declined and made a face. "Doesn't look appetizing."

Tina laughed. Another guest at the table glowered at Mary.

"Before we announce this year's Platinum Pen Award winner..."

Announcements faded to white noise as Myaisha focused on the Palmetto Writers table.

Tullulah Bishop radiated poise and confidence. Her streaked blond hair had been fashioned into an elaborate bouffant. A 1950s-style plate hat perched precariously on the side of her head.

Joyce frequently inspected the contents of her tote bag, resting it lovingly on her lap. Rhonda sat between Tullulah and Joyce, chatting intermittently with Tullulah, who looked disinterested.

As Mrs. Rohrshack invited volunteers to the stage in thanks for their participation, Myaisha spied two entrants slipping in from a rear door. She gasped.

"What?" Tina asked, spinning around to follow Myaisha's gaze. "Look."

"Who is it?" Mary asked, lowering her voice.

"Alice and Tad." Myaisha scooted her chair away from the table to get a better view.

Volunteers descended from the stage and regained their seats. During this intermission, Alice and Tad maneuvered to the front table and joined the Palmetto Writers.

Despite the intervening distance, Myaisha noticed gawks and stares from the group members. A flushed Alice introduced Tad to people at the table. Then she shimmied a chair between Joyce and Rhonda. Tad moved his chair slightly aside away from the table. Tullulah shot Alice surreptitious glances.

"I wish I could be near their table," Myaisha said.

"Me too." Tina giggled. "Tullulah looks pissed."

About to make a comment, the man next to Mary followed their gazes and observed the Palmetto Writers table too. He said, "Tullulah should have invited Alice. Paige did so much for the Charleston writing group, despite the venom in her blog."

Tina asked him, "You've read Paige's blog?"

"Oh, yes." He scooted closer to the table. "I live in Summerville, but I've occasionally attended the Palmetto Writers meetings." His nose twitched. "And let me tell you, those meetings are a hotbed of gossip."

"Really." Myaisha listened, keeping an eye on the Palmetto Writers.

"They would be all smiles while besmirching each other online with petty reviews and trolling."

"No way." Tina slid closer to Myaisha to hear better as the man lowered his voice.

"If someone left Tullulah a bad review, Joyce would gather the ladies together and push the review off the platform."

Tina and the gentleman continued their cross-table conversation as Newson accepted the microphone. "Fiction Writers of America values transparency. Therefore, I will explain the contest rules and selection process for the Platinum Pen Award."

"You know Joyce is an editor," the man said.

"I attended her book editing class," Tina said.

He nodded. "She has good insight. Before moving to South Carolina, I believe she worked for a big five publishing house in New York."

Myaisha frowned. "Major step down in career."

Mary asked, "Couldn't she work remotely and keep her position?"

"She still works for a New York publisher," another person at the table said. "Now will y'all please be quiet."

The man looked down his bulbous nose. "Rude."

"This is about socializing and networking," Myaisha said.

"I want to hear about the selection process," the woman snapped back.

"Newson is reading directly from their website." Tina pulled out her cellphone and showed the woman. "You can see it anytime."

The woman hesitantly read off Tina's phone. "Why waste our time?" In a tizzy, the woman gobbled her dinner.

Whispering, Mary said, "I'm glad we ate barbecue earlier."

Vinson had succeeded Newson at the microphone. He spoke about membership enrollment and welcomed new writers' groups from around the country to their first conference.

"Time for our preeminent event," Mrs. Rohrshack said, stripping Vinson of the microphone.

He swiftly retreated off to the side while Newson retrieved a package from the edge of the platform.

"It is with great pleasure that I announce this year's Platinum Pen Award winner." Mrs. Rohrshack accepted a large gold envelope from Mrs. Newson. The former peeled open the envelope.

Silence engulfed the room, as if everyone held their breath.

Myaisha stole a glance at Tullulah Bishop.

Was she already rising?

Mrs. Rohrshack gaped expectantly. "And the winner—"

"Excuse me, ladies and gentlemen." A short woman, barely over five feet, strode onto the stage.

The auditorium erupted in applause. Thirty or more people stood, clapping and hooting.

In reply to Myaisha's frown, Tina said, "Lydia Keller, President of Fiction Writers of America."

Mrs. Rohrshack's eyes bulged. Crimson and shaking, she ceded the microphone to Mrs. Keller while clutching the envelope. As if disciplining a recalcitrant child, Mrs. Keller plucked the envelope from the vice president's grasp.

"Good evening." Mrs. Keller had difficulty getting the audience to settle. "Thank you for such a warm reception." She gazed across the room with a firm jaw and dark black eyes.

Mrs. Keller struck Myaisha as neither a fool nor a person to mince words.

"I must apologize for my absence. Administrative matters required my presence, and my flight landed late in Charlotte. Fortunately, I arrived on cue."

For some time, Mrs. Keller thanked the board members and volunteers.

Light sparkled off the golden envelope. Lydia Keller said, "This year, Fiction Writers of America will *not* be awarding a Platinum Pen Award."

Murmurings reached a feverish pitch.

"Please listen." Keller raised her hands. "This is important."

Myaisha's eyes bounced from the Palmetto Writers table to the administration members.

Vinson inched off stage.

Mrs. Keller swallowed. "Questions have been raised about the Platinum Pen Award procedure. Concerned members have brought discrepancies to my attention."

Vinson had completely abandoned the stage platform. He stealthily wormed his way toward a side exit. With attendees focused on the president, Myaisha doubted anyone appreciated his actions.

"Fiction Writers of America wants—no, must—ensure our award process is without fault."

Applause drowned out her words.

"After consulting counsel, I hired an accounting firm to review our processes and procedures. Our website will be updated with names of each award judge, including their profiles."

Tullulah blanched. Her plate hat slipped off her towering locks onto the table.

The president continued, "Going forward, Fiction Writers of America will ensure judges have no past or present business rela-tionships with contest entrants."

More applause with a few shouts of approval.

Mrs. Keller raised her chin and looked across the room. "I want each and every member to take pride in our processes and to know that the Platinum Pen Award is above reproach."

Audience members stood with thunderous applause.

In the excitement, Myaisha struggled to observe Vinson or the Palmetto Writers' table. Though her cellphone rang, she ignored it, eager to keep an eye on certain people.

By the time audience members regained their seats, Vinson had disappeared.

Chapter 32

President Keller re-established a modicum of decorum. Some people left, but most remained. Attendees bombarded Keller with questions, which bounced around the chaotic room.

Between chatter and questions, Myaisha's head ached. "I'll catch up later." She started to leave when Tina grabbed her wrist.

"Where are you going?"

Myaisha's cellphone rang again. "I have to get this."

Tina nodded and released her.

On her way out of the room, Myaisha glanced at the table for the Palmetto Writers. Half the people had departed.

Where did everyone go?

As the doors to the conference room closed behind her, Myaisha answered the cellphone. "Yes?"

"We've been calling," Todd said. "Where have you been?"

"The award ceremony."

"Is an award ceremony more important than Paige's murder?"

She ignored his sarcasm and focused on the last word. "I thought the police ruled it an accident."

A second voice came over the line. It took a second for Myaisha to recognize the voice.

Detective Salter said, "An official statement regarding Mrs. Goodson's death was scheduled for release on Monday. It will be amended."

Myaisha asked, "Why?"

"The lipstick in the tote bag contained arsenic."

All three remained silent for a moment.

"So, whether the book contained poison or not—"

"Someone intended to kill Paige," Myaisha said, finishing the detective's sentence.

"Once we conclude our investigation, the DA will decide to charge murder or attempted murder."

"I see." Myaisha considered this new piece of information.

A steady stream of people exited the conference room. She moved to an area with minimal traffic.

"Again. I'm sorry about the tote bag. It wasn't my intention to impede your investigation."

"All good," the detective said. "Actually, I'm on my way over. I want to nail down parts of your statement."

"No problem." She considered where to meet. "There's quite a ruckus downstairs."

"Oh?" Todd asked.

"Are you coming?" She realized her statement might have sounded... Needy? "I can speak to you both at the same time—if it's convenient."

They arranged to meet in the hotel suite upstairs. She hung up.

Gathering her bearings, Myaisha considered where everyone went. And by everyone, she meant Vinson, Alice, Tad, Tullulah, Joyce, and Rhonda.

Mrs. Keller's statement sent shockwaves throughout the room, but the immediate absconders were from the Palmetto Writers table and the committee membership chair.

What is Vinson's connection to the Palmetto Writers, and why would he fear an audit?

Vinson became visibly alarmed upon Mrs. Keller's arrival. But the comment about an independent audit made him flee. Why?

As chair of the membership committee, he had no direct interaction with the award process. Or did he?

FWA had been less than transparent with their award selection process. Perhaps he participated in a way unknown to the administration. Initially, Paige contacted him with her concerns before going to the FWA president.

Had Vinson murdered Paige to hide shenanigans with the Platinum Pen Award? If he had, why?

Money, power, prestige.

Though unpublished, Myaisha understood the enormous power editors and publishing houses held over authors—and future authors. Vinson published his first book years ago. A scandal would limit his future opportunities.

Myaisha noticed a familiar, unwelcome figure approaching. She admired the woman's unique design aesthetic.

Lynn wore a dressy pantsuit with a diminutive top hat. "Good stuff, huh?"

"Depends upon your perspective."

"For a true crime author, it's pure gold." With a gap-toothed grin, Lynn departed.

The hotel lobby held no answers. Myaisha wanted to ditch the heels aching her feet and rest. For over three minutes, she waited in front of the elevators. "This is ridiculous." She opted to take the stairs.

By the fourth floor, she realized how out of shape she had become. Winded, she rested against the cement wall.

Voices echoed from a higher floor. Trickles of conversation reached her.

"I'm not doing this on my own," someone said.

"You're messing with the wrong person. I'll destroy you," a second person replied.

With a burst of energy, Myaisha raced upstairs. She reached the next floor as a door shut, sending a loud boom ringing down the stairwell. Fatigued, she took the next flight at a slower pace. At a slog, she took each step with a deep inhale.

Halfway up the next flight, she noticed a solo drop of blood in the middle of a gray step. Myaisha skirted the blood and heard a distinct dripping.

Drip. Drip.

Perturbed, she struggled up to the seventh floor. In shock, she clutched the railing.

Vinson's head dangled off a stairstep. Blood oozed from a wound in the back of his head, dripping down the cold, stone steps. Myaisha didn't need to check a pulse. She immediately dialed 911.

Chapter 33

Police personnel were packed inside the narrow stairway. Mobile flood lights illuminated Vinson's ashen face. Shadowed corners of the stairwell cast eerie glows.

Myaisha flattened herself against the wall, hoping to disappear into one of those corners.

Between finding two bodies and carrying Paige's tote bag around, Rock Hill Homicide will suspect me of murder.

Other than glaring at her upon his arrival, Detective Cambell gave her a wide berth. His partner, however, questioned Myaisha for at least half an hour. Detective Salter checked pictures and texts on her cellphone.

"I didn't call anyone except 911," she insisted for the umpteenth time.

His chin stiffened. "Not even your writing group."

"No. One." She folded her arms over her chest and leaned against the wall. For another half hour, she waited as forensics collected evidence.

Once preliminaries had been completed, Detective Salter escorted her to a tiny room off the lobby. Police had cordoned off other conference rooms to question guests.

Detective Salter held out a chair for Myaisha. He and Todd rested on opposite sides of the table. The former flipped open a notepad.

"From the beginning."

Myaisha exhaled. "I am not repeating myself."

Detective Salter glowered. "Do you understand the trouble you're in?"

"I'm done." She rose.

Todd uncrossed his legs and reached for her hand.

She pulled away. "This is ridiculous. I've told you multiple times that I took the stairs because the elevators were occupied."

"You expect me to believe a meddlesome amateur detective with nothing better to do in her life than to interfere in police investigations just happened to find the body of a murder suspect in a stairwell?"

"Since when was Hunter Vinson a murder suspect?" Myaisha squeezed the table as if needing support. "I had no idea the police suspected him, especially since I had only been informed moments before that Paige Goodson's death was considered a homicide."

She started to leave, then spun around. "I have been nothing but cooperative with the Rock Hill police. From the moment Paige Goodson died, I have shared everything I knew or suspected. And you dare to harass me—"

"Harass. Lady—"

"It's Dr. Douglas." She threw her shoulders back. "Now, I'm tired. After I leave the lobby, I'm going upstairs to shower and go to sleep. If the police have further questions, they can ask nicely or contact my attorney."

Detective Salter reached forward. Myaisha braced, prepared to be restrained. Instead, he extended his hand, which she accepted.

"Have a nice evening, Doctor."

She gave a slight nod and departed. Furious at the detective's treatment, Myaisha entered the elevator without noticing Todd at her side. Once the elevator doors closed, she slumped against the wall.

"Tired?" he asked.

Tears brimmed in her eyes.

"Come here." He gave her a side hug. "Don't get upset."

Her chest caved. "I'm so tired...and stupid."

He thinks this is about Vinson, but I miss Deniece. I can't do this alone.

"It's fatigue." He squeezed her shoulder. "I would describe you as impetuous, with a nasty habit of stumbling across corpses. But never stupid."

"I did want to know where Vinson went," she said, wiping her eyes. "But I didn't believe he was in danger."

"Did you suspect him?"

She paused momentarily.

Todd leaned away from her a bit. "Are you considering telling me a lie?"

"No." Myaisha frowned. "I'm trying to assess how I really felt."

The elevator doors opened and deposited them on the eleventh floor. Todd escorted her to the suite.

"Want to come in?"

His head tilted. "Dare I?"

Myaisha squeezed his arm. "I'm exhausted, but talking will help me calm down enough to sleep."

"Are your roomies back?"

The door popped open, and Tina dragged Myaisha inside. "We've been waiting."

Not finding Mary in the living room, Myaisha asked, "We?"

"Okay, me." Tina dropped onto the couch beside Myaisha. "Why didn't you call?"

Tina noticed Todd and grinned. "Should've known you'd call him before me."

"Technically, I called Rock Hill police." Kicking off her shoes, Myaisha reclined into the couch cushions. "Todd came along for moral support."

Tina checked her watch. "It's been hours since the body was discovered."

"And how do you know, Mrs. de Jesus?" Todd asked.

"I talked with the hotel staff." Her mouth downturned. "Don't tell Ian."

"Yes, ma'am." Todd rested on the corner of the desk.

Myaisha yawned.

He said, "You need sleep."

"Once I get these thoughts out of my head, I can rest."

"It must be murder inside your brain."

Tina giggled and winked at him.

"At least one person values my humor."

She yawned again. "I'll value it more after sleep."

Todd stretched his legs along the multicolored carpet. "Speak your peace, woman."

"Okay." Myaisha inhaled deeply and glanced at Tina. "Will you take notes?"

Tina positioned a laptop on the coffee table. "Let it rip."

Giving Tina a side glance, Myaisha reviewed the evening's events.

"President Keller was speaking on stage when Hunter Vinson snuck out of the ballroom. I left because Todd called." Myaisha's lips snapped shut.

Did he want to keep the announcement about Paige's death being an official homicide secret?

She glanced at him, but he acted oblivious to her concern. At the moment, Myaisha decided not to share it.

"After Todd called, I wanted to go to my room and consider what I'd learned."

Todd leaned forward. "Forget why you left. Tell us what worried you."

She reflected. "Half the people at the Palmetto Writers table had left."

"Who?" Tina asked, not looking up from the keyboard.

"Let me see." Myaisha chewed her bottom lip. "Alice, Tad, Joyce, Rhonda, and Tullulah."

Tina perked up. "Tullulah."

"I know." Myaisha stifled a yawn. "Surprised me, too."

"Did you see her silly hat?" Tina laughed. "Her hairdo was an even worse monstrosity."

"I liked the hat."

Todd's finger snaps caught their attention. "Can we focus? Two murders outweigh an ugly hat."

Myaisha pouted. "The hat wasn't ugly."

"There was another murder?" Tina gawked.

"He's referring to Paige."

In answer to Tina's wrinkled forehead, Myaisha explained, "The police initially believed arsenic from the book caused Paige's death. But—"

"Umm hmm." Todd loudly cleared his throat.

"Apologies." In an aside to Tina, Myaisha said, "New evidence led homicide to reclassify Paige's death."

"And you know about this evidence, but won't tell me?" Tina gazed imploringly at her.

Myaisha tilted her chin toward Todd.

He said, "Mrs. de Jesus, an active investigation is taking place. It takes priority over..." He hesitated.

Myaisha appreciated his reticence. Tina's recent obsession with true crime writing bordered on maniacal.

"Over literary concerns."

Tina's body sagged, but she gave no protest.

"The elevators were taking an excessive amount of time." Myaisha considered the point.

Could the delayed elevators be related to Vinson's murder? A ploy to delay discovery of the body?

She rejected the idea. In the stairwell, Myaisha heard two people arguing. The murder was likely impulsive.

"I waited a while."

"It must have been a long time for you to take the stairs." Tina chuckled.

"Watch it."

Todd walked into the kitchenette for some water. He handed Myaisha a glass. "What next?"

"Like I told Detective Salter, I heard voices."

"But you couldn't distinguish them," Todd said.

"One was a woman's voice, the other..." Myaisha chugged half a glass of water. "I couldn't identify the other."

"Voices in the stairwell might be unrelated to Vinson's death," Tina said, "since you couldn't tell their direction."

"True." Todd returned to the desk chair.

"They came from above me." Myaisha sipped more water. "But I couldn't swear to which floor."

"It's unlikely the conversation you relayed occurred separately from Vinson's murder," Todd added. "That would be an extraordinary coincidence."

"I heard blood dripping before I reached the body."

"Eww." Tina's shoulders flinched.

"It was ghastly."

"Did you touch him?" Todd asked.

"Not at first. I called 911, then checked him." Myaisha swallowed the remaining water. "He had sustained a head injury to the occiput. The way his head dangled over the edge of the step prevented me from doing CPR."

"Move him and risk a spinal injury or delay CPR," Tina said while typing notes.

"Exactly."

"What did you notice around the area?" Todd asked, as if disinterested in the medical implications.

"Blood on the fire extinguisher box."

"Box?" Tina asked.

"The fire extinguishers in the stairwells are housed in glass boxes."

"Was blood on the actual fire extinguisher?" Todd asked.

She shrugged. "I didn't open the case to examine the extinguisher."

"It was closed?" Todd and Tina asked simultaneously.

"Yes."

Todd frowned. "But you noticed drops of blood on the steps below his body."

Myaisha said, "I did."

"How did they get there?"

All three stared at each other.

"The dead guy didn't place them there."

"Dramatic music. Someone else was present when Vinson got hit," Tina said.

"In other words, the killer," Todd said.

Chapter 34

Sunlight peeked around the curtained window with a foreboding glow. Myaisha reached over to the side table and checked her cellphone. No calls from Deniece. She sniffled and trudged into the shower.

Fifteen minutes later, Myaisha entered the shared living room suite and found Tina hunched over a laptop. "Morning."

"There's a membership meeting at nine in the Empire Conference Room." Tina remained focused on the keyboard.

"I won't make it."

"Oh." Like a bird, Tina's head perked up and tilted slightly. "Something's up?"

Unsure about sharing her thoughts, she said, "I need to reflect on what we've gathered."

"Sounds indecisive." Tina returned to typing.

Early in that morning, Myaisha reached an epiphany. Yesterday, she, Tina, and Todd discussed the case long into the night. Sleep hit her like a sledgehammer.

At dawn, she arose and relieved herself. With a lighter bladder, blood flooded her brain along with a myriad of scenarios concerning Paige's death.

Myaisha hesitated to share her insights. Desperation made Tina careless. She didn't want suppositions about a murder to end up in Tina's true crime novel.

After all, she could be wrong. Once, Myaisha had made a terrible error about a murderer, and it nearly ended with her demise. Shaking those thoughts away, Myaisha prepared to brew tea.

Knock, knock.

"You expecting someone?"

"Maybe Deniece forgot her key." The slight lilt in Tina's reply made Myaisha cringe.

"Are you suggesting—"

Knock, knock.

She dismissed the comment and headed for the door.

How can I judge Tina when I suspected my best friend of infidelity?

"Good morning." Mary popped out of the second bedroom. "Ready for another busy day?"

The knocking persisted with a heavier tone. Myaisha hurried to the door while Mary and Tina discussed their plans.

"About time." Todd handed her a tray of beverages. "The coffees are probably cold by now. I got you a chai tea."

"Thanks." She placed the refreshments on the diminutive coffee table.

Todd reclined on the couch after setting a box on the table. "Donuts. The fuel of detecting."

"How like a cop," Mary said, helping herself to coffee and a glazed confection.

Minutes passed as they ate and conversed about lighter topics. Above the chitchat, Myaisha considered whether to inform Todd of her intentions or to forge forward alone.

Alone.

No more Easy Rawlins and Mouse, and it was her fault.

I knew how deeply committed Deniece and Barry were. Why did infidelity become a possibility in my mind?

Because a role-playing sexual tryst between a married couple would have never occurred to her.

Deniece was right. I am sanctimonious.

Could she change? Should she?

She jolted from Tina's hands clapping in front of her face.

"Earth to Myaisha," Tina said. "Where were you?"

"Thinking over the day's activities," Myaisha lied.

Tina shut down her laptop and slid it into a carrying case. "I plan to be in the front row for the Fiction Writers of America meeting this morning."

"You want to see if they address Vinson's death?" Myaisha asked, tying her sneakers.

"They have to." Tina buttoned up her sweater. "Two murders and questions about their award selection process."

Mary brightened. "I will be attending the poet's corner. They asked me to read one of my poems."

"Congratulations." Myaisha gave Mary a hug. "They'll be delighted."

"Hope so," Mary said before departing.

"Want to join me?" Tina asked, hovering beside the doorway.

Myaisha shook her head. "I have other tasks to complete."

"Like finding our missing roommate." Tina left with a devilish glint in her gaze.

The door barely shut before Todd rose. "What are your plans?"

Can I trust him?

"I'll tell you, but..." She studied his profile for a moment. "Come with me, but don't interfere."

His jaw clenched. "I'm listening."

"Promise."

Todd stayed silent. Half a minute of the staring game elapsed before Myaisha caved.

"Fine." She dashed into the bedroom and grabbed her purse. "You can call Detective Salter if you wish, but let me speak with her first."

Todd's brow creased. "Who?"

Myaisha exited the room with him on her heel.

"Where are we going?" Todd asked.

As they rushed inside the elevator, he said, "I can't help if you don't tell me where we are going."

She peered at him from the corner of her eye. "If I tell you what I have in mind, you'll try to talk me out of it."

He scratched his head. "Being your sidekick is dangerous."

The elevator pinged, and they exited the cab.

"At least it's not boring." She grinned.

Myaisha knocked on the door. A quarter of a minute elapsed before it flew open.

"Oh, it's you," Joyce said, pinching her lips. "I don't have time right now." She exited the room and circled around Myaisha.

"I understand, but the Rock Hill police may not." She waited beside the door. "They'll be curious about your haste to leave."

Joyce pivoted around. "What are you talking about?" Her gaze bore into Myaisha.

"Paige's death and the theft of a rare, valuable book."

A greenish tinge crept across Joyce's cheeks. She swallowed. Her mouth opened, but no words came out.

"Do you understand now?" Myaisha's left brow arched.

Tremulous, Joyce swiped the card key over the reader. "Come inside."

Myaisha preceded Todd. He shot her a quick questioning glance, which she ignored.

Lights popped on as Joyce circled around the room. She collapsed on the couch. A tote bag rested beside her leg.

Todd remained in the hallway near the door. Myaisha brought a chair opposite Joyce.

"The temptation must have been tremendous. You're not a thief by nature."

"Humph." Joyce perched on the edge of the couch. Her hands twisted and untwisted on her lap. "I'm not so sure."

"Did you plan to steal the book, or was it an impulse?"

"When I heard about Paige's death…" Joyce's voice wavered. She squeezed her hands together and took a deep breath. "Impulse. Believe me. I never stole anything in my life."

"How did you contact the dealer?" Myaisha asked, noticing Todd reaching for his cellphone. She gestured with her hand for him to wait.

"Paige didn't hide her side business selling rare books—at least not from me." Joyce sat on her hands. "Alice knew about it too, but Paige wouldn't allow her little sister to be tainted with anything nefarious."

"Who's the dealer?"

Joyce regarded her for a moment, straightening her back. "I can't—won't—divulge their name. These people have money and influence."

Myaisha nodded in agreement. Rock Hill police might choose to pursue the case, but she didn't insist.

Joyce's shoulders slumped. "How did you figure it out?"

"I noticed the books you purchased. Hardback books cost twenty-five to thirty dollars each. Expensive for a librarian on a limited income."

"Yeah. Not smart."

"I adore books, too."

Joyce gazed out of the window. "It's always been my dream to have a huge personal library." She returned to squeezing her hands together. "I'll lose my job. Will I go to jail?"

Todd said, "Theft pales in comparison to Paige's death."

In a flurry, Joyce leaped off the couch. "I didn't kill her."

"Who did?" Todd asked.

With her mouth gaping, Joyce gawked at Myaisha and Todd. "I...I don't know. It must have been someone from Fiction Writers of America."

Myaisha joined Joyce beside the window. "Why would they kill Paige?"

"Because of the contest."

"Do you have any evidence of their involvement?" Todd asked. "Or are you simply diverting scrutiny from your culpability?"

Joyce's cheeks blushed a deeper red than her lipstick. "I did not kill Paige."

"But you stole from her," Todd asserted.

"*After* I heard about her death."

"There's no way to prove you stole the book after Mrs. Goodson's death without confirmation from the buyer. Tell me when you transferred possession of the book."

"I gave them the book on Friday," Joyce said, raising her chin.

"The authorities will need to speak with the buyer to confirm your story." Myaisha watched Joyce trembling.

The librarian's voice waffled. "Not possible. The buyer would be livid." She slumped against the wall.

Myaisha guided her to a nearby chair. "For what it's worth, I don't believe you killed Paige."

A forlorn look sparked in Joyce's eyes.

"But I'm not the police."

To get Joyce off the suspects list, Myaisha would need to find the murderer.

Chapter 35

A second after they left Joyce's hotel room, Todd directed Myaisha down a side hallway.

"I have to call Salter," Todd whispered as guests walked by.

Her shoulders stiffened. "Why?"

His dour face gave a silent reply.

"The police must be told. I understand. But why now?"

"Because he's my friend and a fellow cop."

Myaisha considered their options. "Can't you wait until—"

Todd pulled out his cellphone. "Ben? I have something for you."

Though the bar was closed for drinks, Myaisha, Todd, and Detective Salter gathered there to discuss new developments.

Only a few days prior, Myaisha had witnessed Deniece chatting with an unknown man. A man she had suspected of carrying on an illicit affair with her dearest friend.

Idiot.

"Thanks for the call," Salter said, seated facing the doorway.

Myaisha sat across from him. Todd occupied the remaining chair.

"So," the detective removed a notepad from his coat breast pocket, "this Joyce woman stole a valuable book."

Simultaneously, Todd said, "Yes," and Myaisha said, "But she didn't murder Paige."

The detective frowned. "How do you know?"

She reflected a moment. "The theft was spontaneous, but the murder had been coordinated. The poisoner placed arsenic in Paige's lipstick, which required premeditation." Myaisha let those comments sink in.

"I meant, how do you know Joyce didn't plan to murder Goodson and steal the book?" Detective Salter countered.

Myaisha sat ramrod straight. "During the conference, I noticed Joyce buying books. Lots of books."

Both Todd and Detective Salter regarded her questioningly.

"If Joyce plotted to murder Paige and steal this rare book, what was her exit strategy?"

"Hmm." Todd drummed his fingers along the table.

"Joyce drove up to Rock Hill with other members of the Palmetto Writers group. How would she explain a large cache of books on their return trip to Charleston?"

Patiently, she awaited a response.

"Members of her writing group knew Joyce worked as a librarian on a modest salary. Suddenly, she's flush with cash. Wouldn't that look suspicious?"

Detective Salter shrugged. "She's a stupid murderer. We see those types all the time."

"Stupid in executing a theft but brilliant about the poisoning mechanism?"

Todd smacked the table with a palm. "Exactly. It's been bothering me the entire time."

Myaisha agreed. "When Paige died, no one suspected murder. Given her extensive medical history of diabetes and end-stage renal disease, Paige's death would have been tragic but not criminal."

"But what about her accusations surrounding the writing group?" Detective Salter asked. "People would've questioned the circumstances of her death."

"Perhaps, but not to any significant degree."

"Other than a bothersome mystery writer from Greensboro, no one else cared." Todd smirked.

"Let me see." Detective Salter inhaled deeply. "The murderer planned to disguise Paige's death as a complication of her medical condition."

"Correct." Myaisha nodded.

"And the theft of the books—"

"Was incidental to the murder," Todd finished.

"An opportune moment for a weak woman." Myaisha watched Detective Salter, gauging whether he had been persuaded.

He held her gaze a moment before saying, "I don't know. Joyce, as the murderer and thief, is simpler. Most murders, I find, are straightforward."

"Not Myaisha murders," Todd joked.

She glared at him.

Detective Salter rose. "I appreciate the information." He addressed Todd. "I'll update the chief. Let him know where things stand."

Todd stood, and they shook hands.

"What should we do next?" Myaisha asked.

"We?" Detective Salter returned the notepad to his coat pocket. He made a circle with his finger. "There is no we. This ends here." He stabbed the table with an index finger. "Stop investigating. Go back to your writing conference."

He strode away. At the entrance to the bar, he swung around. "Have a happy life. And if we don't meet again, I know I'll have one." He left.

Myaisha folded her arms over her chest. "Unnecessarily rude."

Todd laughed. "He figured you out with one murder."

"I'm trying to help."

"You're a doctor, not a cop. Go heal someone." He laid a hand on her shoulder. "And stay out of it. Salter has all the information. It's up to the authorities."

"They're wrong. Joyce is not a murderer."

Todd shook his head. "You're not going to stop, are you?"

A twinkle lit in Myaisha's eyes.

Chapter 36

Myaisha's cellphone buzzed. She turned her back to Todd while answering.

"Hello?"

"Mya, I'm leaving."

"Why?" She walked away from Todd, lowering her voice. "I'm so sorry. Please—"

"I left the key to the SUV in the hotel room," Deniece said. "Drive safely."

The call ended.

"D?" Myaisha stared at the blank screen. She dialed the number twice, but each time the call went to voicemail. "Damn."

How am I going to fix this?

She jumped as a hand squeezed her shoulder.

Todd said, "Everything okay?"

"Forget it."

He studied her face. "Bad news?"

Myaisha shook her head. "Personal problems."

"I have plenty of those."

She stared at the cellphone.

How do I mend things with Deniece?

Todd squeezed her arm. "You good?"

"Will be."

His weighty gaze showed he doubted the veracity of her statement. Myaisha patted his hand.

"Deniece and I are having a disagreement."

"Don't tell me the fabulous detective duo has split?"

Tears gathered in Myaisha's eyes.

"Hey, I'm sorry." He rubbed her arm. "Is it serious?"

Myaisha caught a tear before it dripped down her cheek. "I hope not."

Together, they exited the bar.

"Can I give you a ride?"

Unsure of his meaning, her forehead wrinkled.

"Back to Greensboro. I need to leave." Todd glanced at his watch. "Things to finish around the house before work tomorrow."

Myaisha gave him a short hug. "Thanks for coming. I really appreciated it."

He smiled. "Someone has to look after you."

Myaisha remained in the lobby after Todd left. She hoped to catch Deniece on the way out. They must have left before she called.

Dazed, Myaisha wandered around the lobby. Beside the Clayton "Peg Leg" Bates Conference Room, she spotted Rhonda and Tullulah. She headed over.

With bent heads, the women conferred, scrutinizing anyone nearby. About five feet away, Tullulah spotted her.

Rhonda glanced up. Pancake makeup tainted her usually spotless skin. Tullulah hadn't abandoned her blood-red lipstick.

Tacky.

Both women turned their backs to Myaisha. She hesitated for a moment, then dismissed the idea of speaking with them.

The police suspected Joyce of murdering Paige. The librarian had stolen an expensive book, which gave credence to Salter's position. But Myaisha had known several murderers—unfortunately—and their behavior fit a pattern. People, in general, acted within certain parameters.

Stealing a book fit with Joyce's character, impulsive and sly. The poisoning, however, had been methodical and cruel. Death by arsenic would be painful. The murderer hated Paige with a ferocity that disregarded the safety of other people.

What if Alice borrowed Paige's lipstick? Or Paige might have regifted it. Another person might easily have been injured or killed.

This murderer wanted Paige to suffer. Joyce lacked that depth of passion, except for books.

The killer took time to understand Paige's habits. Lipstick as a vehicle to deliver poison required personal knowledge of an individual. For instance, Myaisha rarely wore makeup, and lipstick even less often.

Alice mentioned a party in Charleston right before the conference. Could the lipstick have been a birthday gift?

And what about Hunter Vinson? How did his murder relate to Paige's? If it did.

Myaisha couldn't ask Detective Salter, since he had ordered her to stay out of his investigation. On the other hand, Detective Cambell had been blatantly hostile. He would be a definite no.

Todd had returned to Greensboro. Besides, she preferred not to work too closely with him.

Why not?

Because it felt comfortable, and she didn't want to blur the lines of their friendship.

Myaisha wanted Deniece back, but she had messed up.

How do you recover from suspecting your best friend of infidelity?

Chapter 37

Myaisha glanced up as Tina and Mary hustled across the bustling lobby, weaving around departing visitors.

"Where've you been?" Tina asked, tucking several wayward strands of hair behind her ear.

"Todd and I—"

"The closing ceremony was amazing!" Mary said. "I met a poet from Barbados. She's published three poetry books."

"Forget about the poet." Tina drew Myaisha closer. "The Fiction Writers of America president explained what's going on with the Platinum Pen Award."

Myaisha allowed Tina to guide her to the elevators. The latter explained the morning conference with the FWA president.

Tina said, "They hired a New York law firm to review their judging procedures. Mrs. Keller personally apologized to this year's contest entrants and refunded all fees."

Myaisha's mouth opened, but Tina continued.

"They even took questions."

"Bet that was interesting," Mary said.

"Unbelievable." Tina's arms moved animatedly as she spoke. "Several people asked about Vinson's death. Even Lynn asked a few questions."

Myaisha listened closely to Tina's account. "What did the president say?"

Their conversation ceased as the elevator doors opened. They exited as a gaggle of people flooded inside the cab. Not until they entered their suite did the conversation resume.

Myaisha hurried to the bedroom she shared with Deniece, hopeful of seeing her friend. Other than an unmade bed, the room looked similar to when she had left that morning. She retrieved the SUV keys from the bedside table.

Sitting on the edge of the bed, she phoned Deniece. Again, the call went to voicemail. Myaisha's head sagged. She startled from a knock on the door.

"Ready to go?" Mary asked.

"Coming." Myaisha packed her suitcase and scanned the room for anything missing. On the closet floor, she found one of FWA's complimentary tote bags. A gift for new members.

Must have belonged to Deniece.

Gifted. Gifts.

"Birthday."

"Hey," Tina said, popping her head inside the bedroom. "Time to go. Sunday checkout is at noon. We don't want to pay a late fee."

Reflective, Myaisha entered the sitting area. Her thoughts flowed over the many conversations she'd had during the conference. Piecemeal, an idea blossomed. In the background, she heard Tina and Mary conversing, but her thoughts circled around Paige's murder.

Paige *and* Vinson. Two murders. Perhaps it was the heat or being outside of Greensboro, but she'd been dense.

Myaisha forgot to ask Detective Salter if he believed the murders were connected. Not that it mattered, because she knew the truth. But she didn't have evidence. Detective Salter could find it.

Tina snapped her fingers. "Myaisha?"

Mary touched her arm. "You've been acting strange all weekend."

"I know. It's been difficult."

"Where's Deniece?" Mary asked, observing the SUV keys in Myaisha's hand.

"Off on a rendezvous." Tina's eyebrows wiggled suggestively.

"Don't say that! Deniece would never cheat on Barry!" Myaisha shouted.

"Whoa, whoa," Tina said. "No one mentioned cheating."

"Deniece and Barry like role-playing," Mary tittered.

Myaisha frowned. "How did you know?"

"Who doesn't?" Tina lifted her suitcases and headed for the door.

"Have you read any of her books?" Mary followed Tina. "Those books make me feel like a virgin, and I have three kids."

Everyone recognized Deniece and Barry's romantic play but me?

Resigned, Myaisha turned off the lights and exited the suite.

"This has been exciting," Tina said. "I finished my book synopsis and emailed my agent."

"You think they'll accept it?" Mary asked.

"They should. It's good." Tina entered the elevator and pressed the lobby button. "We don't have a resolution yet, but I constructed a sound beginning premise."

Mary chuckled. "For once, a murder Myaisha couldn't solve."

"Oh, I solved it."

The elevator doors opened as Mary and Tina gawked.

In the registration checkout line, Tina tugged on Myaisha's shirt. "Tell me."

"I became fixated with Joyce's…" Realizing they were surrounded by people, Myaisha lowered her voice. "A type of romantic suspense surrounded the theft of a rare toxic book. I let it distract me from the facts."

"You're going to have to explain," Tina said after turning in their room keys.

Mary strutted away from them toward the exit. "Where's the car? I'm not interested in murders or rigged contests."

"Tina!"

They spun around as Lynn bore down upon them.

Panting and readjusting her glasses, Lynn caught up with them beside the revolving door.

"Oh, hey, Lynn," Tina said with an obvious lack of enthusiasm.

"Did you consider my proposal?"

"I did."

Lynn's eyes opened expectantly. Myaisha and Mary shared a questioning glance.

Blushing, Tina said, "Sounds good."

"Awesome!" Lynn gave Tina a quick hug. "I have to run. My ride's waiting. My agent will call yours."

Tina nodded.

"Bye, partner." In a swirl of energy, Lynn swept out the revolving doors and into a sedan parked under the hotel's portico.

In tandem, Myaisha and Mary turned toward Tina.

"We're collaborating on the story."

"Why didn't you tell us?" Myaisha asked.

"I didn't want you guys to think I crapped out."

"Crapped..." Mary shook her head. "Tina, a collaboration with another author makes perfect sense."

Myaisha agreed.

Tina's shoulders relaxed. "Thanks. I wasn't sure how it would appear."

"Girl, you're crazy," Mary said, pinching Tina's arm. "A book with Lynn will open you up to her readers."

"Precisely what I was thinking," Tina said. "It will increase my audience. And those readers might buy my first book."

Outside the hotel, Tina secured a trolley while Myaisha waited for their parking stub to be validated.

Mary tugged on Myaisha's shirt and pointed. "Look."

In the parking lot, two Rock Hill patrol cars idled in the Carolina sun. Straining against the glare, Myaisha spotted Joyce in the rear of one of the cars. She abandoned her suitcases and strode over to the detectives.

Along the way, Myaisha noticed Detective Cambell's jaw tense. "Detective—"

"Go away!" he boomed. "This is an official investigation."

Inside the patrol car, Joyce sobbed with her hands cuffed behind her back.

"You're making a mistake."

"This ain't Greensboro."

"No doubt."

The detective sneered. "I'll lock you up and tie so many complaints to your ass, you'll be lucky to get out by Thanksgiving."

Detective Salter intervened, addressing his partner. "Cool it. People are watching."

To Myaisha, he asked, "What now?"

"Joyce isn't a murderer."

"I listened to your supposition. The chief didn't agree." The detective's shoulders squared. "Leave before you're arrested for interfering with an investigation."

"I'm trying to save Rock Hill from an embarrassing charge of unlawful detainment."

A smirk crossed the detective's face. "How are we unlawfully detaining anyone? We can hold a suspect for theft while building a murder charge."

Myaisha's chin thrust forward. "And who did she steal from?"

"From Paige Goodson."

"Did Mrs. Goodson report this theft?"

A shadow darkened the detective's face. "You told me about the theft."

"But I can't accuse Joyce of stealing something which didn't belong to me."

"The sister—"

"Won't file charges because she doesn't want the authorities to learn about Paige's tax-free book-selling enterprise."

"Are you telling me we can't make a theft charge stick?"

Myaisha shrugged. "Not without Joyce implicating herself."

Detective Salter's nostrils flared. He escorted Myaisha by her elbow to a shaded area on the side of the hotel. Tina and Mary joined them, dragging an assortment of luggage.

"Do we have to include the entire Greensboro writing group?"

"Wait in the car." She handed Tina, who had begun removing her laptop from its case, the key.

"This... I need this for my story," Tina whispered into Myaisha's ear.

The detective's hands clenched.

"I'll explain everything on the drive home." Myaisha shooed Tina and Mary away.

Tina grumbled but headed for the parking garage with Mary.

Near the hotel's entrance, Myaisha noticed Rhonda and other members of the Charleston writing group departing.

She pointed the detectives toward the Palmetto Writers. "I suggest you speak with those ladies before they leave Rock Hill."

A minute elapsed as Detective Salter conferred with his partner.

Myaisha watched as they escorted three members of the Palmetto Writers group toward a second police car.

She hovered a foot behind the detectives.

"On what authority are you detaining us, Detective?" Tullulah asked, rose-colored splotches blooming across her freckled chest.

"We have a few questions," Detective Salter said. "With your cooperation, this will be wrapped up in no time."

Tullulah snorted.

"If this is about Paige's death," another member of the Charleston writing group said, "we have nothing to add to our earlier comments."

Detective Salter glanced at Myaisha, and she stepped forward.

"Did you all attend Paige's birthday party last month?" she asked.

"Are you kidding?" Tullulah chuckled. "It's hot as Hades out here, and you're asking about a party?" She looked past Myaisha at the detective. "Are we under arrest?"

"No one is under arrest, *yet*," Detective Cambell said, scowling at Myaisha.

"Why is Joyce in a patrol car?" Rhonda asked, wiping sweat from her brow.

"Outrageous!" Tullulah glared down her twittering aquiline nose. "I demand to call my attorney. This is false imprisonment."

"You're not in prison, ma'am," Detective Salter said.

"This is embarrassing." Tullulah thrust her shoulders back. "To be publicly questioned by the police."

"Would you rather answer questions downtown?" Detective Salter asked. "We'd be happy to escort you inside one of our air-conditioned patrol cars."

Tullulah's red-lacquered lips trembled.

Myaisha came forward and faced Tullulah. "This will be the least of your embarrassments."

"How dare you? I'm a successful published author. Winner of the—"

"The Fiction Writers of America audit will reveal *how* you won the Platinum Pen Awards. Won't it, Rhonda?" Myaisha asked

"Why ask me? I have no idea what an audit might reveal."

"Time for chapter and verse, Easy Rawlings." Detective Salter retreated a step and invited Myaisha to proceed.

"Alice mentioned a birthday party for Paige in Charleston."

She pivoted toward the detectives. "Remember, Paige became ill *prior* to the conference. Therefore, the poisoning must have started in Charleston."

"Crazy fool," Rhonda said, tossing her blond hair aside.

The demarcation between her porcelain skin and her foundation became more evident in front of her hairline.

"Forensics will prove it from Paige's hair and blood samples. They also—"

Myaisha paused, catching a glint from Detective Salter's gaze. Apparently, the police wanted to keep the lipstick secret.

"Police have identified the source of the poison. A gift from you at the birthday party."

"Prove it." Rhonda advanced on Myaisha. Her teeth clenched. "Prove I poisoned Paige."

"Alice attended the birthday party. She'll remember who gave which gifts."

"Another psycho true crime aficionado." Her gaze swept over Myaisha. "Probably never published." Rhonda leered into Myaisha's face. "And never will."

Don't play her mind games. Stick to facts.

"The point is motive."

Rallying, Rhonda rested her hand on her hip. "And what motive did I have to kill Paige?"

Tullulah joined Rhonda's side. "Paige accused Fiction Writers of America of improprieties, not us."

Myaisha said, "Those improprieties involved the Platinum Pen Award judging process."

"I've never been a judge," Tullulah said.

"But Rhonda has."

Rhonda's body appeared to shrink a bit.

"Didn't you work in New York before moving to Charleston?" Myaisha asked.

"And?" Rhonda crossed her arms over her chest. "I'm no longer employed by a New York publisher."

"Through this former employer, you worked on Tullulah's books. Did you explain these prior collaborations to the award committee?"

A sickly green tinge peeked from behind Rhonda's concealer.

"Hunter Vinson suspected something was awry when Tullulah repeatedly won the award."

"I had nothing—"

"Shut it," Detective Cambell said, suddenly interested.

Tullulah quieted, tapping her foot against the asphalt.

Myaisha glanced momentarily at the detective, who gave her a thumb's-up.

"Before joining Fiction Writers of America, Vinson had a writing career in New York. As a Fiction Writers of America board member, he had access to the list of judges. He recognized Rhonda's name and knew about her prior career with a major New York publishing house."

Rhonda snorted. "Supposition."

"Details can be substantiated. Though you convinced Tisha Newson, probably with bribes, to keep the list of judges off the organization's website, Vinson remained uncomfortable. He valued his reputation."

"Just because I worked in publishing doesn't mean I did anything illegal."

"Whether or not cheating to help Tullulah win the Platinum Pen Award is criminal will be determined by a court of law. However, in the court of public opinion, it would be a death blow to Tullulah's career."

"How are you going to prove any of this...this nonsense?" Tullulah glowered. "I'll sue you and the Rock Hill police force."

"Truth is the best defense." Myaisha sized her up. "Besides, rumor will kill your career faster than the police could make a charge."

Detective Salter nodded in agreement.

Tullulah trembled. Her finger darted in Myaisha's face. "You wouldn't."

"True. I would not."

The bleached-blond author exhaled. "I didn't think so."

"But Paige would have."

Rhonda's corner lip curled in a sneer. "Pompous witch."

"Hypocritical given her under-the-table book-selling business," Myaisha added in a rare moment of consensus.

"How true." Rhonda ran her fingers along her blond hair. "Dogmatic and preachy. Paige acted so superior. Like she had such impeccable ethics."

"How did you learn about Paige's meeting with the president?" Myaisha asked.

"Hunter."

"He was skittish."

Rhonda's cackle chilled Myaisha despite the South Carolina noon day heat.

"Coward. He worried Lydia Keller would find out."

"The Fiction Writers of America president," Myaisha said in answer to Detective Salter's glance. She turned toward Rhonda. "That's why you killed him."

"I didn't. It was—"

"Shut up!" Tullulah demanded. "We're in enough trouble because of you."

"Me? This is all because of you." Rhonda's eyes narrowed to slits. "Your stupid competition with Paige."

Tullulah snatched Rhonda's wrist. "I'm warning you."

Rhonda smacked Tullulah aside. "Seeing your career burn might be worth it."

Detective Salter stepped between the women and asked Myaisha, "How does this involve Mr. Vinson?"

Myaisha addressed Rhonda. "On the first day of the conference, I admired your impeccable skin, not a blemish to be seen." She peered closer, examining Rhonda's face. "The foundation covers the bruise, but with a court order, homicide will match your blood to that on the stair steps."

"Her?" Detective Cambell asked.

"Like she started to say, Hunter's death was an accident," Myaisha explained. "They argued. I believe he struck her in the face, which explains her sudden need for foundation."

Rhonda darted toward Myaisha, but Detective Salter caught her before the women connected.

Detective Cambell cleared his throat and led Rhonda toward the second patrol car. "You have the right to."

"Just drive me downtown," Rhonda said. "I have no comment."

As the patrol car drove off, Myaisha smiled at Detective Salter.

"You're still irritating," he said.

"Glad to help."

He laughed. "Go home, Doc."

Chapter 38

The SUV glided off Interstate 85 onto Highway 29 toward Greensboro. Myaisha signaled and moved behind an eighteen-wheeler into the slow lane.

"And you discovered the killer from a birthday gift?" Tina asked while jotting down notes.

"It was the totality of the evidence."

Mary said, "Joyce didn't strike me as a murderer."

"My impression also. Which is why I returned to motive."

Tina typed and asked, "Joyce used the murder to hide her theft?"

"More like she saw an opportunity. With Paige dead..." Myaisha paused while passing a semi-trailer. "Joyce knew Alice couldn't alert the authorities to the theft without acknowledging Paige sold books without declaring the income."

Tina frowned. "How did you connect Paige's murder to Vinton's?"

"I didn't at first."

"Not until you found the lipstick, right?" Mary asked from the rear seat.

"The central question remained how Paige ingested the poison," Myaisha said.

"Poison is the perfect weapon for a distance killing," Tina said, not looking up from her laptop.

"I thought Alice was involved," Mary said.

Myaisha observed her from the rearview mirror. "Alice feared the police would discover Paige's side hustle. But like Tad said, she didn't participate in the actual business."

"Will the police charge Alice?" Mary asked.

Tina snapped the laptop closed. "With what?"

Mary's brow knitted.

"She's right." Myaisha signaled and exited the highway. "If Alice and Joyce remain silent, the authorities have no evidence to charge them."

"They could alert the IRS." Mary smirked.

Myaisha turned into her cul-de-sac. "True."

As the SUV headed toward her house, Myaisha glanced left at Mrs. Lula's house. A light flickered over the empty porch.

Mrs. Lula needs to change that bulb.

Myaisha parked in her driveway. Mary and Tina exited the car and removed their luggage.

Tina packed the sedan. "Amazing. This came together because you accidentally picked up Paige's tote bag."

"I was slow understanding this murder," Myaisha said. "When I questioned Rhonda, she stated I should leave things to the police. But homicide had been careful not to alert anyone to their suspicions. They had quietly approached me and Deniece. So how did Rhonda know they were investigating?"

Mary hopped into the passenger seat of Tina's car.

Myaisha explained, "Lynn learned about the investigation from her contacts in the Rock Hill Police Department, but how did Rhonda know—"

"Unless she'd been involved," Mary added.

Tina said, "Considering the circumstances, I think you did well."

Poking her head out of the car window, Mary said, "Stop sleuthing. It's bad for your health."

Tina honked and drove off.

After sending a text to AJ and Deniece, Myaisha dropped her luggage inside the house. For a second, she expected Boomer to come bounding forward, forgetting he was with AJ.

Emptiness echoed around the house. On impulse, she left and walked over to Mrs. Lula's house.

Minutes passed without an answer to her knocking. Myaisha peeked inside a front window, but blinds blocked her view. She checked around the outside of the home but detected no movement inside.

The octogenarian valued her privacy and independence, but Myaisha feared she might need assistance.

"Mrs. Lula wouldn't leave the front light on during the day."

She dug inside her pants pocket. Last year, Mrs. Lula gave her a key for emergencies. Myaisha unlocked the door and tiptoed inside.

"Mrs. Lula," she called out. "Hello. It's Myaisha. I noticed your front light bulb needs changing."

She entered the living room. "Mrs. Lula."

Landscape pictures dotted the walls of the immaculate cottage home, but no personal pictures—not even of Mrs. Lula herself. In fact, nothing intimate filled the space. A visitor could discern little about the occupant except how they possessed a fanatical need to clean. Myaisha ran a finger over the coffee table.

No dust or crumbs.

Finding nothing on the first floor, Myaisha began to climb the stairs.

"What are you doing in here?"

Surprised, Myaisha lost her footing and slipped on the first step. She rubbed her bruised shin.

"I called out, but you didn't answer."

Mrs. Lula charged forward. "I wasn't home." Scowling, she eyed Myaisha. "Why did you come inside? I told you not to enter unless it was an emergency."

"The front light was flickering. You're usually fastidious about the house, so I worried something happened to prevent you from changing the bulb."

The senior ignored Myaisha's explanation. Her body trembled. Anger rolled off her like heat from a charcoal grill.

Myaisha presented the key. "Here."

Mrs. Lula's chest heaved as she snatched it from Myaisha's fingers. She circled around Mrs. Lula and headed for the door.

"Wait." Mrs. Lula's face softened. "I'm sorry. I...I don't like people in my house."

"I meant no disrespect. If the light wasn't flickering, I wouldn't have entered."

Mrs. Lula rubbed Myaisha's arm. "You're a good person."

She smiled. Those simple words held a lot of significance. Mrs. Lula was sparse with compliments.

Handing the key back to Myaisha, Mrs. Lula escorted her to the door. "Keep this." Her fingers shook. "It might come in handy soon."

The door closed in Myaisha's face.

Chapter 39

The sun dipped low in the Carolina sky. As if on cue, mosqui-
toes swarmed looking for fresh meat. Myaisha walked home
briskly but confused. Though pleased with Mrs. Lula's kind praise,
the abrupt dismissal made her wonder.

What had Mrs. Lula meant about me needing the key soon?

She dwelled on the problem for only a second because she noticed
an SUV idling at the curb near her mailbox. From the driver's seat,
Barry waved. In a flash, he drove away.

Myaisha raced to the house as Deniece's SUV reversed down
the driveway. Close enough to touch the car, Myaisha signaled for
Deniece to stop.

"D." She grabbed the door handle. "We have to talk."

The window scrolled down. "No, we don't."

"Please." Tears swelled in Myaisha's eyes. "I'm so sorry."

Deniece laughed. "You are so obtuse."

Myaisha flinched.

"Is our friendship so fragile, you believe I wouldn't forgive you?"

"Well, I—"

"Believed I would make a mistake and destroy my marriage for a weekend booty call." Deniece reached through the car window and tugged on a lock of Myaisha's thick mane. "I love you, and I'll forgive you for believing I would ever cheat on Barry."

"I didn't know about your..." Myaisha struggled to choose the right word.

"Role-playing is exciting." Deniece raised her brows suggestively. "Try it some time."

As she reversed down the driveway, Deniece said, "And it's safer than investigating murders." With a laugh, she departed.

Myaisha had barely managed to empty her suitcase when the doorbell rang.

Todd smiled and presented a package. "I come bearing gifts."

She invited him inside.

Hesitant, Todd scanned the foyer. "Where's Cujo?"

She smacked his arm. "Boomer is a sweet dog."

"Yeah, sure."

A familiar aroma tickled her nose. She peeled off the packaging and examined the confections. "Chocolates. Delicious. Thank you."

They settled on the couch facing the backyard.

"I found this chocolatier in Charlotte and picked up a couple boxes."

Myaisha inhaled the fruity aromas. "Mm."

"It fills you up simply from the smell."

"Knowing how you love chocolates, I appreciate your parting with a box."

He chuckled. "It wasn't easy."

An awkward moment passed before Myaisha faced Todd. "I..." She swallowed and stiffened her shoulders. "I need to ask you something."

Todd frowned. "Sure. What's up?"

She set the box down. "I like you, Todd."

He held up a finger. "Let me stop you."

"This is important."

"Wait." He stood. "Before either of us says something embarrassing, let me explain."

"Friends don't have to be embarrassed to share their emotions."

Todd placed a hand on each of her shoulders. "Myaisha, I don't have those feelings for you."

She gaped. "No?"

His head shook. "Afraid not."

Myaisha glanced at the box. "And the gift?"

"A simple gesture for a friend who shares my passion for chocolate."

She collapsed on the couch. "I'm such a fool."

"Not at all." He rested beside her. "We've shared awkward situations before. I should've made my position clearer."

"This isn't you." Her head bowed. "I make presumptions."

"You have good instincts."

She considered the recent assumptions she had made about Deniece.

"In medicine and murder, but not in relationships."

Todd squeezed her hand. "If I was interested in a relationship, you would be top of my list."

"Are you in a relationship?"

He laughed. "Forever curious."

Myaisha grinned mischievously. "Between friends."

"I'm happily asexual."

Her brow puckered. "Which means?"

"I'm not interested in sexual intimacy."

"Have you ever..."

How did she ask politely about his sexual predisposition? Certain things she found easier to ask patients than friends.

"I have been involved in sexual and intimate relationships in the past, but not currently."

"Past. Todd, you're in your thirties."

He rose. "And delighted to be uninvolved."

At the front door, Myaisha gave him a hug. "I'm glad we're friends."

Todd kissed her cheek as the front door opened.

Chapter 40

A tense moment passed as AJ entered the foyer, accompanied by Boomer and Zoey. The brown Lab bounded into the house. Boomer growled and eyed Todd.

The police detective slipped behind Myaisha with his gaze locked on the black Lab.

AJ dropped the leashes and hovered in the doorway. Myaisha dashed over and gave him a peck on the lips. He failed to respond, cemented to the doorway.

Boomer barked and advanced toward Todd.

"Down," Myaisha ordered.

The Lab quizzically regarded her as if asking why he shouldn't attack this intruder.

"Now, Boomer."

Continuing to eye Todd, the Labrador heeled.

Myaisha picked up the leashes.

Todd inched behind Myaisha, as far away from Boomer as physically possible. "I'll be leaving."

At the door, he held out his hand toward AJ. "Nice to see you again."

The firefighter hesitated for a moment before accepting Todd's gesture. He didn't speak but merely inclined his head.

Myaisha placed the leashes in the laundry room and filled the dogs' food and water bowls. While washing up in the sink, she asked AJ, "Was everything okay? Did Boomer behave?"

The Lab glanced at AJ before returning to his food bowl.

"Things here were fine." He set a bouquet of flowers on the kitchen island.

"Oh, they're beautiful." Myaisha picked up the flowers and rushed around the island to give AJ another kiss. This time she noticed his lackluster response. "Something wrong?"

"You tell me." His gaze swept over her.

"Tell you what?"

His head angled toward the front door. "About him."

"Todd?"

"Yeah, the detective."

She smiled. "AJ."

"Don't make fun of me."

Myaisha gave him a long bear hug and kissed him deeply on the lips. "I'm not."

AJ placed his hands around her waist. "And the cop."

She guided him to the living room couch. "A friend."

"Why is he always over here?"

She held up the box of chocolates from Todd. "Because we both love crime and chocolate, though not in the same order."

AJ reclined on the couch. Myaisha curled up along his side.

"I apologize for being jealous."

"Don't. I made several miscalculations myself this weekend."

His forehead creased.

"I have a...a blind spot when it comes to relationships."

"Oh?"

"Unimportant." Myaisha caressed his neck and kissed his cheek. "What matters is, we understand how we feel about each other."

The Labradors trotted out the sliding glass doors. Leaves on the magnolia trees shimmered. Birds sang and dashed around tree limbs.

Myaisha inhaled, adoring the scent of wood and musk along AJ's neck.

He kissed her temple. "Like the flowers?"

"Not nearly as much as the man who gave them to me."

They shared a deep, passionate kiss.

Myaisha twisted the curls in AJ's afro around her fingers. "Do you ever desire a more adventurous relationship?"

He pulled her onto his lap. "What did you have in mind?"

She kissed his eyelids. "Role-playing. Dressing up. Pretending to be other people."

AJ sighed. "How about I wear my helmet and chase you around the house?"

Laughing, Myaisha slid off his lap and turned on the record player. "What are you in the mood for?"

"I'm more of a Al Green *Love and Happiness* than Prince's *Let's Go Crazy.*"

"Understood."

They cuddled on the couch as Al Green crooned throughout the house.

About the author

Though born in Illinois, as a military dependent, Michelle moved between San Diego, California and Charleston, South Carolina. She enrolled at the University of California Santa Cruz before attending Michigan State University to complete a pediatric residency program. After over twenty years in clinical medicine, Michelle now works as a medical consultant. As a member of Crime Writers of Color, Sisters in Crime Capitol Crimes, Authors Guild, ALLi, and Science Fiction Writers of America, her writing interests cover many genres—mystery, paranormal, and thrillers.

In 2025, Michelle won the Next Generation short story award for The Riddle Inheritance. That same year, she received Nashville Silver Falchion Judge's Top Picks in the cozy mystery category for Murder Between Neighbors. If not writing, she will be outside gardening or bicycling.

Thank you for reading *Murder at the Writers Conference.* As a self-published author, I depend upon reviews to increase my visibility and credibility. Please post an honest review. Visit my website for book reviews and resources for readers and writers.

If you missed the other books in the series, read *Murder Is Revealing, Murder In Gemini*, and *Murder Between Neighbors*. Sign up for my Write Club Mysteries newsletter and receive bonus content, information on new releases, and resources from the writing community.

For those who enjoy thrillers, read *Hollow Voices*, a psychological thriller.

Mwindaji is for paranormal and horror readers. Check out *Dark Blood Awakens* and *Dark Blood Curse*.